比较文学与世界文学 研究丛书

主编 曹顺庆

二编 第 **27** 册

英文阅读与古诗英译（上）

张 智 中 著

花木兰文化事业有限公司

国家图书馆出版品预行编目资料

英文阅读与古诗英译（上）／张智中 著－－初版－－新北市：
花木兰文化事业有限公司，2023〔民112〕
序2+ 目6+120 面；19×26 公分
（比较文学与世界文学研究丛书 二编 第27 册）
ISBN 978-626-344-338-9（精装）
1.CST：中国诗 2.CST：翻译
810.8   111022130

ISBN-978-626-344-338-9

9 786263 443389

比较文学与世界文学研究丛书
二编　第二七册　　　　　　　ISBN：978-626-344-338-9

英文阅读与古诗英译(上)

作　　者　张智中
主　　编　曹顺庆
企　　划　四川大学双一流学科暨比较文学研究基地
总 编 辑　杜洁祥
副总编辑　杨嘉乐
编辑主任　许郁翎
编　　辑　张雅淋、潘玟静　美术编辑　陈逸婷
出　　版　花木兰文化事业有限公司
发 行 人　高小娟
联络地址　台湾 235 新北市中和区中安街七二号十三楼
　　　　　电话：02-2923-1455 ／传真：02-2923-1452
网　　址　http://www.huamulan.tw 信箱　service@huamulans.com
印　　刷　普罗文化出版广告事业
初　　版　2023 年 3 月
定　　价　二编 28 册（精装）新台币 76,000 元　　版权所有 请勿翻印

英文阅读与古诗英译（上）

张智中 著

作者简介

张智中，南开大学外国语学院教授、博士研究生导师、翻译系主任，中国翻译协会理事，中国英汉语比较研究会典籍英译专业委员会副会长，天津师范大学跨文化与世界文学研究院兼职教授，天津市比较文学学会理事，天津市人民政府学位委员会评议组成员、专业学位教育指导委员会委员，国家社科基金项目通讯评审专家和结项鉴定专家，天津外国语大学中央文献翻译研究基地兼职研究员，《国际诗歌翻译》季刊客座总编等。已出版编、译、著 100 余部，发表学术论文 110 余篇，曾获翻译与科研多种奖项。汉诗英译多走向国外，获国际著名诗人和翻译家的广泛好评。译诗观：但为传神，不拘其形，散文笔法，诗意内容；将汉诗英译提高到英诗的高度。

提　　要

　　《英文阅读与古诗英译》融理论与实践于一体，包括理论篇和实践篇。理论篇包括"英文阅读与古诗英译"、"读者定位与译者的英文阅读"、"古诗英译的语言策略"、"读英文，译古诗"、"英译汉：同词异译的启发——以 warm, faint, gather 为例"、"汉译英：同词异译的启发——以'爱好''喜欢''由于''总之'为例"、"古典诗词断句英译"、"以古诗英译为目的的英文阅读"等八个小节，进行理论阐述，并结合一些翻译的实例，来说明古诗英译过程中，英文阅读对于译者的重要性。实践篇包括 150 首古诗英译，译诗以唐宋诗词为主，也包括少量唐宋之前的作品（如《诗经·采薇》），唐宋之后的作品（如明代徐渭的《题葡萄图》、清代郑燮的《竹石》），以及现当代诗词（如鲁迅的《自嘲》，毛泽东的《七绝·为女民兵题照》和《十六字令三首》等），均为经典诗作。每首译诗，都结合阅读积累的相关英文表达或句子，并将其化用在译诗之中。有时结合作者不同时期的译诗，分析如何改进，有时一诗多译，平行并列，有时比较他人译文，以凸显英文阅读之重要性。诗歌是艺术，诗歌翻译也是艺术；诗歌是语言的艺术，诗歌翻译也是语言的艺术。而语言的艺术，只有起点，没有终点。因此，从事古诗英译者，必须养成日复一日终其一生的英文阅读习惯，才有望把中国古诗英译的事情做好，为中华诗词在英语世界的传播做出切实的贡献。

夜　吟

陆游

六十余年妄学诗，
功夫深处独心知。
夜来一笑寒灯下，
始是金丹换骨时。

Composing Poems in the Depth of Night

Lu You

Infatuated with poetry for over sixty years,
my consummate writing skills are privy
to none. Under a cold lamp in such
a cold night, I smile to myself,
glorying in a sudden
enlighten-
ment.

To Classical Chinese Poetry

Following the roads
of dream to you, my feet
never rest. But one glimpse of you
in the English world would be
worth all these many days,
all these nights
of love.

(Zhang Zhizhong)

比较文学的中国路径

曹顺庆

自德国作家歌德提出"世界文学"观念以来，比较文学已经走过近二百年。比较文学研究也历经欧洲阶段、美洲阶段而至亚洲阶段，并在每一阶段都形成了独具特色学科理论体系、研究方法、研究范围及研究对象。中国比较文学研究面对东西文明之间不断加深的交流和碰撞现况，立足中国之本，辩证吸纳四方之学，而有了如今欣欣向荣之景象，这套丛书可以说是应运而生。本丛书尝试以开放性、包容性分批出版中国比较文学学者研究成果，以观中国比较文学学术脉络、学术理念、学术话语、学术目标之概貌。

一、百年比较文学争讼之端——比较文学的定义

什么是比较文学？常识告诉我们：比较文学就是文学比较。然而当今中国比较文学教学实际情况却并非完全如此。长期以来，中国学术界对"什么是比较文学？"却一直说不清，道不明。这一最基本的问题，几乎成为学术界纠缠不清、莫衷一是的陷阱，存在着各种不同的看法。其中一些看法严重误导了广大学生！如果不辨析这些严重误导了广大学生的观点，是不负责任、问心有愧的。恰如《文心雕龙·序志》说"岂好辩哉，不得已也"，因此我不得不辩。

其中一个极为容易误导学生的说法，就是"比较文学不是文学比较"。目前，一些教科书郑重其事地指出：比较文学不是文学比较。认为把"比较"与"文学"联系在一起，很容易被人们理解为用比较的方法进行文学研究的意思。并进一步强调，比较文学并不等于文学比较，并非任何运用比较方法来进行的比较研究都是比较文学。这种误导学生的说法几乎成为一个定论，

一个基本常识，其实，这个看法是不完全准确的。

让我们来看看一些具体例证，请注意，我列举的例证，对事不对人，因而不提及具体的人名与书名，请大家理解。在 Y 教授主编的教材中，专门设有一节以"比较文学不是文学比较"为题的内容，其中指出"比较文学界面临的最大的困惑就是把'比较文学'误读为'文学比较'"，在高等院校进行比较文学课程教学时需要重点强调"比较文学不是文学比较"。W 教授主编的教材也称"比较文学不是文学的比较"，因为"不是所有用比较的方法来研究文学现象的都是比较文学"。L 教授在其所著教材专门谈到"比较文学不等于文学比较"，因为，"比较"已经远远超出了一般方法论的意义，而具有了跨国家与民族、跨学科的学科性质，认为将比较文学等同于文学比较是以偏概全的。"J 教授在其主编的教材中指出，"比较文学并不等于文学比较"，并以美国学派雷马克的比较文学定义为根据，论证比较文学的"比较"是有前提的，只有在地域观念上跨越打通国家的界限，在学科领域上跨越打通文学与其他学科的界限，进行的比较研究才是比较文学。在 W 教授主编的教材中，作者认为，"若把比较文学精神看作比较精神的话，就是犯了望文生义的错误，一百余年来，比较文学这个名称是名不副实的。"

从列举的以上教材我们可以看出，首先，它们在当下都仍然坚持"比较文学不是文学比较"这一并不完全符合整个比较文学学科发展事实的观点。如果认为一百余年来，比较文学这个名称是名不副实的，所有的比较文学都不是文学比较，那是大错特错！其次，值得注意的是，这些教材在相关叙述中各自的侧重点还并不相同，存在着不同程度、不同方面的分歧。这样一来，错误的观点下多样的谬误解释，加剧了学习者对比较文学学科性质的错误把握，使得学习者对比较文学的理解愈发困惑，十分不利于比较文学方法论的学习、也不利于比较文学学科的传承和发展。当今中国比较文学教材之所以普遍出现以上强作解释，不完全准确的教科书观点，根本原因还是没有仔细研究比较文学学科不同阶段之史实，甚至是根本不清楚比较文学不同阶段的学科史实的体现。

实际上，早期的比较文学"名"与"实"的确不相符合，这主要是指法国学派的学科理论，但是并不包括以后的美国学派及中国学派的学科理论，如果把所有阶段的学科理论一锅煮，是不妥当的。下面，我们就从比较文学学科发展的史实来论证这个问题。"比较文学不是文学比较""comparative literature is not literary comparison"，只是法国学派提出的比较文学口号，只是法国学派一派的主张，而不是整个比较文学学科的基本特征。我们不能够把这个阶段性的比较文学口号扩大化，甚至让其突破时空，用于描述比较文学所有的阶段和学派，更不能够使其"放之四海而皆准"。

法国学派提出"比较文学不是文学比较"，这个"比较"（comparison）是他们坚决反对的！为什么呢，因为他们要的不是文学"比较"（literary comparison），而是文学"关系"（literary relationship），具体而言，他们主张比较文学是实证的国际文学关系，是不同国家文学的影响关系，influences of different literatures，而不是文学比较。

法国学派为什么要反对"比较"（comparison），这与比较文学第一次危机密切相关。比较文学刚刚在欧洲兴起时，难免泥沙俱下，乱比的情形不断出现，暴露了多种隐患和弊端，于是，其合法性遭到了学者们的质疑：究竟比较文学的科学性何在？意大利著名美学大师克罗齐认为，"比较"（comparison）是各个学科都可以应用的方法，所以，"比较"不能成为独立学科的基石。学术界对于比较文学公然的质疑与挑战，引起了欧洲比较文学学者的震撼，到底比较文学如何"比较"才能够避免"乱比"？如何才是科学的比较？

难能可贵的是，法国学者对于比较文学学科的科学性进行了深刻的的反思和探索，并提出了具体的应对的方法：法国学派采取壮士断臂的方式，砍掉"比较"（comparison），提出比较文学不是文学比较（comparative literature is not literary comparison），或者说砍掉了没有影响关系的平行比较，总结出了只注重文学关系（literary relationship）的影响（influences）研究方法论。法国学派的创建者之一基亚指出，比较文学并不是比较。比较不过是一门名字没取好的学科所运用的一种方法……企图对它的性质下一个严格的定义可能是徒劳的。基亚认为：比较文学不是平行比较，而仅仅是文学关系史。以"文学关系"为比较文学研究的正宗。为什么法国学派要反对比较？或者说为什么法国学派要提出"比较文学不是文学比较"，因为法国学派认为"比较"（comparison）实际上是乱比的根源，或者说"比较"是没有可比性的。正如巴登斯佩哲指出："仅仅对两个不同的对象同时看上一眼就作比较，仅仅靠记忆和印象的拼凑，靠一些主观臆想把可能游移不定的东西扯在一起来找点类似点，这样的比较决不可能产生论证的明晰性"。所以必须抛弃"比较"。只承认基于科学的历史实证主义之上的文学影响关系研究（based on scientificity and positivism and literary influences.）。法国学派的代表学者卡雷指出：比较文学是实证性的关系研究：“比较文学是文学史的一个分支：它研究拜伦与普希金、歌德与卡莱尔、瓦尔特·司各特与维尼之间，在属于一种以上文学背景的不同作品、不同构思以及不同作家的生平之间所曾存在过的跨国度的精神交往与实际联系。”正因为法国学者善于独辟蹊径，敢于提出“比较文学不是文学比较”，甚至完全抛弃比较（comparison），以防止“乱比”，才形成了一套建立在“科学”实证性为基础的、以影响关系为特征的“不比较”的比较文学学科理论体系，这终于挡住了克罗齐等人对比较文学“乱比”的批判，形成了以“科学”实证为特征的文学影响关系研究，确立了法国学派的学科理论和一整套方法论体系。当然，法国学派悍然砍掉比较研究，又不放弃“比较文学”这个名称，于是不可避免地出现了比较文学名不副实的尴尬现象，出现了打着比较文学名号，而又不比较的法国学派学科理论，这才是问题的关键。

当然，法国学派提出“比较文学不是文学比较“，只注重实证关系而不注重文学比较和文学审美，必然会引起比较文学的危机。这一危机终于由美国著名比较文学家韦勒克（René Wellek）在 1958 年国际比较文学协会第二次大会上明确揭示出来了。在这届年会上，韦勒克作了题为《比较文学的危机》的挑战性发言，对“不比较”的法国学派进行了猛烈批判，宣告了倡导平行比较和注重文学审美的比较文学美国学派的诞生。韦勒克作了题为《比较文学的危机》的挑战性发言，对当时一统天下的法国学派进行了猛烈批判，宣告了比较文学美国学派的诞生。韦勒克说：“我认为，内容和方法之间的人为界线，渊源和影响的机械主义概念，以及尽管是十分慷慨的但仍属文化民族主义的动机，是比较文学研究中持久危机的症状。”韦勒克指出：“比较也不能仅仅局限在历史上的事实联系中，正如最近语言学家的经验向文学研究者表明的那样，比较的价值既存在于事实联系的影响研究中，也存在于毫无历史关系的语言现象或类型的平等对比中。”很明显，韦勒克提出了比较文学就是要比较（comparison），就是要恢复巴登斯佩哲所讽刺和抛弃的“找点类似点”的平行比较研究。美国著名比较文学家雷马克（Henry Remak）在他的著名论文《比较文学的定义与功用》中深刻地分析了法国学派为什么放弃“比较”（comparison）的原因和本质。他分析说：“法国比较文学否定‘纯粹’的比较（comparison），它忠实于十九世纪实证主义学术研究的传统，即实证主义所坚持并热切期望的文学研究的'科学性'。按照这种观点,纯粹的类比不会得出任何结论,尤其是不能得出有更大意义的、系统的、概括性的结论。……既然值得尊重的科学必须致力于因果关系的探索,而比较文学必须具有科学性,因此,比较文学应该研究因果关系,即影响、交流、变更等。"雷马克进一步尖锐地指出,"比较文学"不是"影响文学"。只讲影响不要比较的"比较文学",当然是名不副实的。显然,法国学派抛弃了"比较"(comparison),但是仍然带着一顶"比较文学"的帽子,才造成了比较文学"名"与"实"不相符合,造成比较文学不比较的尴尬,这才是问题的关键。

美国学派最大的贡献,是恢复了被法国学派所抛弃的比较文学应有的本义——"比较"(The American school went back to the original sense of comparative literature ——"comparison"),美国学派提出了标志其学派学科理论体系的平行比较和跨学科比较:"比较文学是一国文学与另一国或多国文学的比较,是文学与人类其他表现领域的比较。"显然,自从美国学派倡导比较文学应当比较(comparison)以后,比较文学就不再有名与实不相符合的问题了,我们就不应当再继续笼统地说"比较文学不是文学比较"了,不应当再以"比较文学不是文学比较"来误导学生!更不可以说"一百余年来,比较文学这个名称是名不副实的。"不能够将雷马克的观点也强行解释为"比较文学不是比较"。因为在美国学派看来,比较文学就是要比较(comparison)。比较文学就是要恢复被巴登斯佩哲所讽刺和抛弃的"找点类似点"的平行比较研究。因为平行研究的可比性,正是类同性。正如韦勒克所说,"比较的价值既存在于事实联系的影响研究中,也存在于毫无历史关系的语言现象或类型的平等对比中。"恢复平行比较研究、跨学科研究,形成了以"找点类似点"的平行研究和跨学科研究为特征的比较文学美国学派学科理论和方法论体系。美国学派的学科理论以"类型学"、"比较诗学"、"跨学科比较"为主,并拓展原属于影响研究的"主题学"、"文类学"等领域,大大扩展比较文学研究领域。

二、比较文学的三个阶段

下面,我们从比较文学的三个学科理论阶段,进一步剖析比较文学不同阶段的学科理论特征。现代意义上的比较文学学科发展以"跨越"与"沟通"为目标,形成了类似"层叠"式、"涟漪"式的发展模式,经历了三个重要的学科理论阶段,即:

一、欧洲阶段，比较文学的成形期；二、美洲阶段，比较文学的转型期；三、亚洲阶段，比较文学的拓展期。我们将比较文学三个阶段的发展称之为"涟漪式"结构，实际上是揭示了比较文学学科理论的继承与创新的辩证关系：比较文学学科理论的发展，不是以新的理论否定和取代先前的理论，而是层叠式、累进式地形成"涟漪"式的包容性发展模式，逐步积累推进。比较文学学科理论发展呈现为层叠式、"涟漪"式、包容式的发展模式。我们把这个模式描绘如下：

法国学派主张比较文学是国际文学关系，是不同国家文学的影响关系。形成学科理论第一圈层：比较文学——影响研究；美国学派主张恢复平行比较，形成学科理论第二圈层：比较文学——影响研究＋平行研究＋跨学科研究；中国学派提出跨文明研究和变异研究，形成学科理论第三圈层：比较文学——影响研究＋平行研究＋跨学科研究＋跨文明研究＋变异研究。这三个圈层并不互相排斥和否定，而是继承和包容。我们将比较文学三个阶段的发展称之为层叠式、"涟漪"式、包容式结构，实际上是揭示了比较文学学科理论的继承与创新的辩证关系。

法国学派提出，可比性的第一个立足点是同源性，由关系构成的同源性。同源性主要是针对影响关系研究而言的。法国学派将同源性视作可比性的核心，认为影响研究的可比性是同源性。所谓同源性，指的是通过对不同国家、不同民族和不同语言的文学的文学关系研究，寻求一种有事实联系的同源关系，这种影响的同源关系可以通过直接、具体的材料得以证实。同源性往往建立在一条可追溯关系的三点一线的"影响路线"之上，这条路线由发送者、接受者和传递者三部分构成。如果没有相同的源流，也就不可能有影响关系，也就谈不上可比性，这就是"同源性"。以渊源学、流传学和媒介学作为研究的中心，依靠具体的事实材料在国别文学之间寻求主题、题材、文体、原型、思想渊源等方面的同源影响关系。注重事实性的关联和渊源性的影响，并采用严谨的实证方法，重视对史料的搜集和求证，具有重要的学术价值与学术意义，仍然具有广阔的研究前景。渊源学的例子：杨宪益，《西方十四行诗的渊源》。

比较文学学科理论的第二阶段在美洲，第二阶段是比较文学学科理论的转型期。从 20 世纪 60 年代以来，比较文学研究的主要阵地逐渐从法国转向美国，平行研究的可比性是什么？是类同性。类同性是指是没有文学影响关系的不同国家文学所表现出的相似和契合之处。以类同性为基本立足点的平行研究与影响研究一样都是超出国界的文学研究，但它不涉及影响关系研究的放送、流传、媒介等问题。平行研究强调不同国家的作家、作品、文学现象的类同比较，比较结果是总结出于文学作品的美学价值及文学发展具有规律性的东西。其比较必须具有可比性，这个可比性就是类同性。研究文学中类同的：风格、结构、内容、形式、流派、情节、技巧、手法、情调、形象、主题、文类、文学思潮、文学理论、文学规律。例如钱钟书《通感》认为，中国诗文有一种描写手法，古代批评家和修辞学家似乎都没有拈出。宋祁《玉楼春》词有句名句："红杏枝头春意闹。"这与西方的通感描写手法可以比较。

比较文学的又一次危机：比较文学的死亡

九十年代，欧美学者提出，比较文学作为一门学科已经死亡！最早是英国学者苏珊·巴斯奈特 1993 年她在《比较文学》一书中提出了比较文学的死亡论，认为比较文学作为一门学科，在某种意义上已经死亡。尔后，美国学者斯皮瓦克写了一部比较文学专著，书名就叫《一个学科的死亡》。为什么比较文学会死亡，斯皮瓦克的书中并没有明确回答！为什么西方学者会提出比较文学死亡论？全世界比较文学界都十分困惑。我们认为，20 世纪 90 年代以来，欧美比较文学继"理论热"之后，又出现了大规模的"文化转向"。脱离了比较文学的基本立场。首先是不比较，即不讲比较文学的可比性问题。西方比较文学研究充斥大量的 Culture Studies（文化研究），已经不考虑比较的合理性，不考虑比较文学的可比性问题。第二是不文学，即不关心文学问题。西方学者热衷于文化研究，关注的已经不是文学性，而是精神分析、政治、性别、阶级、结构等等。最根本的原因，是比较文学学科长期囿于西方中心论，有意无意地回避东西方不同文明文学的比较问题，基本上忽略了学科理论的新生长点，比较文学学科理论缺乏创新，严重忽略了比较文学的差异性和变异性。

要克服比较文学的又一次危机，就必须打破西方中心论，克服比较文学学科理论一味求同的比较文学学科理论模式，提出适应当今全球化比较文学研究的新话语。中国学派，正是在此次危机中，提出了比较文学变异学研究，总结出了新的学科理论话语和一套新的方法论。

中国大陆第一部比较文学概论性著作是卢康华、孙景尧所著《比较文学导论》，该书指出："什么是比较文学？现在我们可以借用我国学者季羡林先生的解释来回答了：'顾名思义，比较文学就是把不同国家的文学拿出来比较，这可以说是狭义的比较文学。广义的比较文学是把文学同其他学科来比较，包括人文科学和社会科学'。"[1]这个定义可以说是美国雷马克定义的翻版。不过，该书又接着指出："我们认为最精炼易记的还是我国学者钱钟书先生的说法：'比较文学作为一门专门学科，则专指跨越国界和语言界限的文学比较'。更具体地说，就是把不同国家不同语言的文学现象放在一起进行比较，研究他们在文艺理论、文学思潮，具体作家、作品之间的互相影响。"[2]这个定义似乎更接近法国学派的定义，没有强调平行比较与跨学科比较。紧接该书之后的教材是陈挺的《比较文学简编》，该书仍旧以"广义"与"狭义"来解释比较文学的定义，指出："我们认为，通常说的比较文学是狭义的，即指超越国家、民族和语言界限的文学研究……广义的比较文学还可以包括文学与其他艺术（音乐、绘画等）与其他意识形态（历史、哲学、政治、宗教等）之间的相互关系的研究。"[3]中国比较文学早期对于比较文学的定义中凸显了很强的不确定性。

由乐黛云主编，高等教育出版社 1988 年的《中西比较文学教程》，则对比较文学定义有了较为深入的认识，该书在详细考查了中外不同的定义之后，该书指出："比较文学不应受到语言、民族、国家、学科等限制，而要走向一种开放性，力图寻求世界文学发展的共同规律。"[4]"世界文学"概念的纳入极大拓宽了比较文学的内涵，为"跨文化"定义特征的提出做好了铺垫。

随着时间的推移，学界的认识逐步深化。1997 年，陈惇、孙景尧、谢天振主编的《比较文学》提出了自己的定义："把比较文学看作跨民族、跨语言、跨文化、跨学科的文学研究，更符合比较文学的实质，更能反映现阶段人们对于比较文学的认识。"[5]2000 年北京师范大学出版社出版了《比较文学概论》修订本，提出："什么是比较文学呢？比较文学是一种开放式的文学研究，它具有宏观的视野和国际的角度，以跨民族、跨语言、跨文化、跨学科界限的各种文学关系为研究对象，在理论和方法上，具有比较的自觉意识和兼容并包的特色。"[6]这是我们目前所看到的国内较有特色的一个定义。

---

1 卢康华、孙景尧著《比较文学导论》，黑龙江人民出版社 1984，第 15 页。
2 卢康华、孙景尧著《比较文学导论》，黑龙江人民出版社 1984 年版。
3 陈挺《比较文学简编》，华东师范大学出版社 1986 年版。
4 乐黛云主编《中西比较文学教程》，高等教育出版社 1988 年版。
5 陈惇、孙景尧、谢天振主编《比较文学》，高等教育出版社 1997 年版。
6 陈惇、刘象愚《比较文学概论》，北京师范大学出版社 2000 年版。

具有代表性的比较文学定义是 2002 年出版的杨乃乔主编的《比较文学概论》一书，该书的定义如下："比较文学是以跨民族、跨语言、跨文化与跨学科为比较视域而展开的研究，在学科的成立上以研究主体的比较视域为安身立命的本体，因此强调研究主体的定位，同时比较文学把学科的研究客体定位于民族文学之间与文学及其他学科之间的三种关系：材料事实关系、美学价值关系与学科交叉关系，并在开放与多元的文学研究中追寻体系化的汇通。"[7]方汉文则认为："比较文学作为文学研究的一个分支学科，它以理解不同文化体系和不同学科间的同一性和差异性的辩证思维为主导，对那些跨越了民族、语言、文化体系和学科界限的文学现象进行比较研究，以寻求人类文学发生和发展的相似性和规律性。"[8]由此而引申出的"跨文化"成为中国比较文学学者对于比较文学定义所做出的历史性贡献。

我在《比较文学教程》中对比较文学定义表述如下："比较文学是以世界性眼光和胸怀来从事不同国家、不同文明和不同学科之间的跨越式文学比较研究。它主要研究各种跨越中文学的同源性、变异性、类同性、异质性和互补性，以影响研究、变异研究、平行研究、跨学科研究、总体文学研究为基本方法论，其目的在于以世界性眼光来总结文学规律和文学特性，加强世界文学的相互了解与整合，推动世界文学的发展。"[9]在这一定义中，我再次重申"跨国""跨学科""跨文明"三大特征，以"变异性""异质性"突破东西文明之间的"第三堵墙"。

"首在审己，亦必知人"。中国比较文学学者在前人定义的不断论争中反观自身，立足中国经验、学术传统，以中国学者之言为比较文学的危机处境贡献学科转机之道。

三、两岸共建比较文学话语——比较文学中国学派

中国学者对于比较文学定义的不断明确也促成了"比较文学中国学派"的生发。得益于两岸几代学者的垦拓耕耘，这一议题成为近五十年来中国比较文学发展中竖起的最鲜明、最具争议性的一杆大旗，同时也是中国比较文学学科理论研究最有创新性，最亮丽的一道风景线。

---

7 杨乃乔主编《比较文学概论》，北京大学出版社 2002 年版。
8 方汉文《比较文学基本原理》，苏州大学出版社 2002 年版。
9 曹顺庆《比较文学教程》，高等教育出版社 2006 年版。

比较文学"中国学派"这一概念所蕴含的理论的自觉意识最早出现的时间大约是 20 世纪 70 年代。当时的台湾由于派出学生留洋学习，接触到大量的比较文学学术动态，率先掀起了中外文学比较的热潮。1971 年 7 月在台湾淡江大学召开的第一届"国际比较文学会议"上，朱立元、颜元叔、叶维廉、胡辉恒等学者在会议期间提出了比较文学的"中国学派"这一学术构想。同时，李达三、陈鹏翔（陈慧桦）、古添洪等致力于比较文学中国学派早期的理论催生。如 1976 年，古添洪、陈慧桦出版了台湾比较文学论文集《比较文学的垦拓在台湾》。编者在该书的序言中明确提出："我们不妨大胆宣言说，这援用西方文学理论与方法并加以考验、调整以用之于中国文学的研究，是比较文学中的中国派"[10]。这是关于比较文学中国学派较早的说明性文字，尽管其中提到的研究方法过于强调西方理论的普世性，而遭到美国和中国大陆比较文学学者的批评和否定；但这毕竟是第一次从定义和研究方法上对中国学派的本质进行了系统论述，具有开拓和启明的作用。后来，陈鹏翔又在台湾《中外文学》杂志上连续发表相关文章，对自己提出的观点作了进一步的阐释和补充。

在"中国学派"刚刚起步之际，美国学者李达三起到了启蒙、催生的作用。李达三于 60 年代来华在台湾任教，为中国比较文学培养了一批朝气蓬勃的生力军。1977 年 10 月，李达三在《中外文学》6 卷 5 期上发表了一篇宣言式的文章《比较文学中国学派》，宣告了比较文学的中国学派的建立，并认为比较文学中国学派旨在"与比较文学中早已定于一尊的西方思想模式分庭抗礼。由于这些观念是源自对中国文学及比较文学有兴趣的学者，我们就将含有这些观念的学者统称为比较文学的'中国'学派。"并指出中国学派的三个目标：1、在自己本国的文学中，无论是理论方面或实践方面，找出特具"民族性"的东西，加以发扬光大，以充实世界文学；2、推展非西方国家"地区性"的文学运动，同时认为西方文学仅是众多文学表达方式之一而已；3、做一个非西方国家的发言人，同时并不自诩能代表所有其他非西方的国家。李达三后来又撰文对比较文学研究状况进行了分析研究，积极推动中国学派的理论建设。[11]

继中国台湾学者垦拓之功，在 20 世纪 70 年代末复苏的大陆比较文学研

---

10 古添洪、陈慧桦《比较文学的垦拓在台湾》，台湾东大图书公司 1976 年版。
11 李达三《比较文学研究之新方向》，台湾联经事业出版公司 1978 年版。

究亦积极参与了"比较文学中国学派"的理论建设和学科建设。

　　季羡林先生 1982 年在《比较文学译文集》的序言中指出："以我们东方文学基础之雄厚，历史之悠久，我们中国文学在其中更占有独特的地位，只要我们肯努力学习，认真钻研，比较文学中国学派必然能建立起来，而且日益发扬光大"[12]。1983 年 6 月，在天津召开的新中国第一次比较文学学术会议上，朱维之先生作了题为《比较文学中国学派的回顾与展望》的报告，在报告中他旗帜鲜明地说："比较文学中国学派的形成（不是建立）已经有了长远的源流，前人已经做出了很多成绩，颇具特色，而且兼有法、美、苏学派的特点。因此，中国学派绝不是欧美学派的尾巴或补充"[13]。1984 年，卢康华、孙景尧在《比较文学导论》中对如何建立比较文学中国学派提出了自己的看法，认为应当以马克思主义作为自己的理论基础，以我国的优秀传统与民族特色为立足点与出发点，汲取古今中外一切有用的营养，去努力发展中国的比较文学研究。同年在《中国比较文学》创刊号上，朱维之、方重、唐弢、杨周翰等人认为中国的比较文学研究应该保持不同于西方的民族特点和独立风貌。1985 年，黄宝生发表《建立比较文学的中国学派：读〈中国比较文学〉创刊号》，认为《中国比较文学》创刊号上多篇讨论比较文学中国学派的论文标志着大陆对比较文学中国学派的探讨进入了实际操作阶段。[14]1988 年，远浩一提出"比较文学是跨文化的文学研究"（载《中国比较文学》1988 年第 3期）。这是对比较文学中国学派在理论特征和方法论体系上的一次前瞻。同年，杨周翰先生发表题为"比较文学：界定'中国学派'，危机与前提"（载《中国比较文学通讯》1988 年第 2 期），认为东方文学之间的比较研究应当成为"中国学派"的特色。这不仅打破比较文学中的欧洲中心论，而且也是东方比较学者责无旁贷的任务。此外，国内少数民族文学的比较研究，也应该成为"中国学派"的一个组成部分。所以，杨先生认为比较文学中的大量问题和学派问题并不矛盾，相反有助于理论的讨论。1990 年，远浩一发表"关于'中国学派'"（载《中国比较文学》1990 年第 1 期），进一步推进了"中国学派"的研究。此后直到 20 世纪 90 年代末，中国学者就比较文学中国学派的建立、理论与方法以及相应的学科理论等诸多问题进行了积极而富有成效的探讨。

---

12 张隆溪《比较文学译文集》，北京大学出版社 1984 年版。
13 朱维之《比较文学论文集》，南开大学出版社 1984 年版。
14 参见《世界文学》1985 年第 5 期。

刘介民、远浩一、孙景尧、谢天振、陈淳、刘象愚、杜卫等人都对这些问题付出过不少努力。《暨南学报》1991 年第 3 期发表了一组笔谈，大家就这个问题提出了意见，认为必须打破比较文学研究中长期存在的法美研究模式，建立比较文学中国学派的任务已经迫在眉睫。王富仁在《学术月刊》1991 年第 4 期上发表"论比较文学的中国学派问题"，论述中国学派兴起的必然性。而后，以谢天振等学者为代表的比较文学研究界展开了对"X+Y"模式的批判。比较文学在大陆复兴之后，一些研究者采取了"X+Y"式的比附研究的模式，在发现了"惊人的相似"之后便万事大吉，而不注意中西巨大的文化差异性，成为了浅度的比附性研究。这种情况的出现，不仅是中国学者对比较文学的理解上出了问题，也是由于法美学派研究理论中长期存在的研究模式的影响，一些学者并没有深思中国与西方文学背后巨大的文明差异性，因而形成"X+Y"的研究模式，这更促使一些学者思考比较文学中国学派的问题。

经过学者们的共同努力，比较文学中国学派一些初步的特征和方法论体系逐渐凸显出来。1995 年，我在《中国比较文学》第 1 期上发表《比较文学中国学派基本理论特征及其方法论体系初探》一文，对比较文学在中国复兴十余年来的发展成果作了总结，并在此基础上总结出中国学派的理论特征和方法论体系，对比较文学中国学派作了全方位的阐述。继该文之后，我又发表了《跨越第三堵'墙'创建比较文学中国学派理论体系》等系列论文，论述了以跨文化研究为核心的"中国学派"的基本理论特征及其方法论体系。这些学术论文发表之后在国内外比较文学界引起了较大的反响。台湾著名比较文学学者古添洪认为该文"体大思精，可谓已综合了台湾与大陆两地比较文学中国学派的策略与指归，实可作为'中国学派'在大陆再出发与实践的蓝图"[15]。

在我撰文提出比较文学中国学派的基本特征及方法论体系之后，关于中国学派的论争热潮日益高涨。反对者如前国际比较文学学会会长佛克马（Douwe Fokkema）1987 年在中国比较文学学会第二届学术讨论会上就从所谓的国际观点出发对比较文学中国学派的合法性提出了质疑，并坚定地反对建立比较文学中国学派。来自国际的观点并没有让中国学者失去建立比较文学中国学派的热忱。很快中国学者智量先生就在《文艺理论研究》1988 年第

---

15 古添洪《中国学派与台湾比较文学界的当前走向》，参见黄维樑编《中国比较文学理论的垦拓》167 页，北京大学出版社 1998 年版。

1 期上发表题为《比较文学在中国》一文，文中援引中国比较文学研究取得的成就，为中国学派辩护，认为中国比较文学研究成绩和特色显著，尤其在研究方法上足以与比较文学研究历史上的其他学派相提并论，建立中国学派只会是一个有益的举动。1991 年，孙景尧先生在《文学评论》第 2 期上发表《为"中国学派"一辩》，孙先生认为佛克马所谓的国际主义观点实质上是"欧洲中心主义"的观点，而"中国学派"的提出，正是为了清除东西方文学与比较文学学科史中形成的"欧洲中心主义"。在 1993 年美国印第安纳大学举行的全美比较文学会议上，李达三仍然坚定地认为建立中国学派是有益的。二十年之后，佛克马教授修正了自己的看法，在 2007 年 4 月的"跨文明对话——国际学术研讨会（成都）"上，佛克马教授公开表示欣赏建立比较文学中国学派的想法[16]。即使学派争议一派繁荣景象，但最终仍旧需要落点于学术创见与成果之上。

比较文学变异学便是中国学派的一个重要理论创获。2005 年，我正式在《比较文学学》[17]中提出比较文学变异学，提出比较文学研究应该从"求同"思维中走出来，从"变异"的角度出发，拓宽比较文学的研究。通过前述的法、美学派学科理论的梳理，我们也可以发现前期比较文学学科是缺乏"变异性"研究的。我便从建构中国比较文学学科理论话语体系入手，立足《周易》的"变异"思想，建构起"比较文学变异学"新话语，力图以中国学者的视角为全世界比较文学学科理论提供一个新视角、新方法和新理论。

比较文学变异学的提出根植于中国哲学的深层内涵，如《周易》之"易之三名"所构建的"变易、简易、不易"三位一体的思辨意蕴与意义生成系统。具体而言，"变易"乃四时更替、五行运转、气象畅通、生生不息；"不易"乃天上地下、君南臣北、纲举目张、尊卑有位；"简易"则是乾以易知、坤以简能、易则易知、简则易从。显然，在这个意义结构系统中，变易强调"变"，不易强调"不变"，简易强调变与不变之间的基本关联。万物有所变，有所不变，且变与不变之间存在简单易从之规律，这是一种思辨式的变异模式，这种变异思维的理论特征就是：天人合一、物我不分、对立转化、整体关联。这是中国古代哲学最重要的认识论，也是与西方哲学所不同的"变异"思想。

---

16 见《比较文学报》2007 年 5 月 30 日，总第 43 期。
17 曹顺庆《比较文学学》，四川大学出版社 2005 年版。

由哲学思想衍生于学科理论，比较文学变异学是"指对不同国家、不同文明的文学现象在影响交流中呈现出的变异状态的研究，以及对不同国家、不同文明的文学相互阐发中出现的变异状态的研究。通过研究文学现象在影响交流以及相互阐发中呈现的变异，探究比较文学变异的规律。"[18]变异学理论的重点在求"异"的可比性，研究范围包含跨国变异研究、跨语际变异研究、跨文化变异研究、跨文明变异研究、文学的他国化研究等方面。比较文学变异学所发现的文化创新规律、文学创新路径是基于中国所特有的术语、概念和言说体系之上探索出的"中国话语"，作为比较文学第三阶段中国学派的代表性理论已经受到了国际学界的广泛关注与高度评价，中国学术话语产生了世界性影响。

四、国际视野中的中国比较文学

文明之墙让中国比较文学学者所提出的标识性概念获得国际视野的接纳、理解、认同以及运用，经历了跨语言、跨文化、跨文明的多重关卡，国际视野下的中国比较文学书写亦经历了一个从"遍寻无迹""只言片语"而"专篇专论"，从最初的"话语乌托邦"至"阶段性贡献"的过程。

二十世纪六十年代以来港台学者致力于从课程教学、学术平台、人才培养，国内外学术合作等方面巩固比较文学这一新兴学科的建立基石，如淡江文理学院英文系开设的"比较文学"（1966），香港大学开设的"中西文学关系"（1966）等课程；台湾大学外文系主编出版之《中外文学》月刊、淡江大学出版之《淡江评论》季刊等比较文学研究专刊；后又有台湾比较文学学会（1973 年）、香港比较文学学会（1978）的成立。在这一系列的学术环境构建下，学者前贤以"中国学派"为中国比较文学话语核心在国际比较文学学科理论、方法论中持续探讨，率先启声。例如李达三在 1980 年香港举办的东西方比较文学学术研讨会成果中选取了七篇代表性文章，以 *Chinese-Western Comparative Literature: Theory and Strategy* 为题集结出版，[19]并在其结语中附上那篇"中国学派"宣言文章以申明中国比较文学建立之必要。

学科开山之际，艰难险阻之巨难以想象，但从国际学者相关言论中可见西方对于中国比较文学学科的发展抱有的希望渺小。厄尔·迈纳（Earl Miner）

---

18 曹顺庆主编《比较文学概论》，高等教育出版社 2015 年版。

19 *Chinese-Western Comparative Literature：Theory & Strategy*，Chinese Univ Pr.1980-6

在 1987 年发表的 *Some Theoretical and Methodological Topics for Comparative Literature* 一文中谈到当时西方的比较文学鲜有学者试图将非西方材料纳入西方的比较文学研究中。(until recently there has been little effort to incorporate non-Western evidence into Western com- parative study.) 1992 年，斯坦福大学教授 David Palumbo-Liu 直接以《话语的乌托邦：论中国比较文学的不可能性》为题 (*The Utopias of Discourse: On the Impossibility of Chinese Comparative Literature*) 直言中国比较文学本质上是一项"乌托邦"工程。(My main goal will be to show how and why the task of Chinese comparative literature, particularly of pre-modern literature, is essentially a *utopian* project.) 这些对于中国比较文学的诘难与质疑，今美国加州大学圣地亚哥分校文学系主任张英进教授在其 1998 编著的 *China in a polycentric world: essays in Chinese comparative literature* 前言中也不得不承认中国比较文学研究在国际学术界中仍然处于边缘地位 (The fact is, however, that Chinese comparative literature remained marginal in academia, even though it has developed closely with the rest of literary studies in the United Stated and even though China has gained increasing importance in the geopolitical world order over the past decades.)。[20]但张英进教授也展望了下一个千年中国比较文学研究的蓝景。

新的千年新的气象，"世界文学""全球化"等概念的冲击下，让西方学者开始注意到东方，注意到中国。如普渡大学教授斯蒂文·托托西（Tötösy de Zepetnek, Steven）1999 年发长文 *From Comparative Literature Today Toward Comparative Cultural Studies* 阐明比较文学研究更应该注重文化的全球性、多元性、平等性而杜绝等级划分的参与。托托西教授注意到了在法德美所谓传统的比较文学研究重镇之外，例如中国、日本、巴西、阿根廷、墨西哥、西班牙、葡萄牙、意大利、希腊等地区，比较文学学科得到了出乎意料的发展（emerging and developing strongly）。在这篇文章中，托托西教授列举了世界各地比较文学研究成果的著作，其中中国地区便是北京大学乐黛云先生出版的代表作品。托托西教授精通多国语言，研究视野也常具跨越性，新世纪以来也致力于以跨越性的视野关注世界各地比较文学研究的动向。[21]

---

20 Moran T．Yingjin Zhang, Ed. China in a Polycentric World: Essays in Chinese Comparative Literature[J].现代中文文学学报,2000,4(1):161-165.

21 Tötösy de Zepetnek, Steven. "From Comparative Literature Today Toward Comparative Cultural Studies." CLCWeb: Comparative Literature and Culture 1.3 (1999):

以上这些国际上不同学者的声音一则质疑中国比较文学建设的可能性，一则观望着这一学科在非西方国家的复兴样态。争议的声音不仅在国际学界，国内学界对于这一新兴学科的全局框架中涉及的理论、方法以及学科本身的立足点，例如前文所说的比较文学的定义，中国学派等等都处于持久论辩的漩涡。我们也通晓如果一直处于争议的漩涡中，便会被漩涡所吞噬，只有将论辩化为成果，才能转漩涡为涟漪，一圈一圈向外辐射，国际学人也在等待中国学者自己的声音。

上海交通大学王宁教授作为中国比较文学学者的国际发声者自 20 世纪末至今已撰文百余篇，他直言，全球化给西方学者带来了学科死亡论，但是中国比较文学必将在这全球化语境中更为兴盛，中国的比较文学学者一定会对国际文学研究做出更大的贡献。新世纪以来中国学者也不断地将自身的学科思考成果呈现在世界之前。2000 年，北京大学周小仪教授发文（*Comparative Literature in China*）[22]率先从学科史角度构建了中国比较文学在两个时期（20世纪 20 年代至 50 年代，70 年代至 90 年代）的发展概貌，此文关于中国比较文学的复兴崛起是源自中国文学现代性的产生这一观点对美国芝加哥大学教授苏源熙（Haun Saussy）影响较深。苏源熙在 2006 年的专著 *Comparative Literature in an Age of Globalization* 中对于中国比较文学的讨论篇幅极少，其中心便是重申比较文学与中国文学现代性的联系。这篇文章也被哈佛大学教授大卫·达姆罗什（David Damrosch）收录于《普林斯顿比较文学资料手册》（*The Princeton Sourcebook in Comparative Literature*，2009[23]）。类似的学科史介绍在英语世界与法语世界都接续出现，以上大致反映了中国学者对于中国比较文学研究的大概描述在西学界的接受情况。学科史的构架对于国际学术对中国比较文学发展脉络的把握很有必要，但是在此基础上的学科理论实践才是关系于中国比较文学学科国际性发展的根本方向。

我在 20 世纪 80 年代以来 40 余年间便一直思考比较文学研究的理论构建问题，从以西方理论阐释中国文学而造成的中国文艺理论"失语症"思考

22 Zhou, Xiaoyi and Q.S. Tong, "Comparative Literature in China", Comparative Literature and Comparative Cultural Studies, ed., Totosy de Zepetnek, West Lafayette, Indiana: Purdue University Press, 2003, 268-283.

23 Damrosch, David (EDT)*The Princeton Sourcebook in Comparative Literature*, Princeton University Press

属于中国比较文学自身的学科方法论，从跨异质文化中产生的"文学误读""文化过滤""文学他国化"提出"比较文学变异学"理论。历经 10 年的不断思考，2013 年，我的英文著作：*The Variation Theory of Comparative Literature*（《比较文学变异学》），由全球著名的出版社之一斯普林格（Springer）出版社出版，并在美国纽约、英国伦敦、德国海德堡出版同时发行。*The Variation Theory of Comparative Literature*（《比较文学变异学》）系统地梳理了比较文学法国学派与美国学派研究范式的特点及局限，首次以全球通用的英语语言提出了中国比较文学学科理论新话语："比较文学变异学"。这一新概念、新范畴和新表述，引导国际学术界展开了对变异学的专刊研究（如普渡大学创办刊物《比较文学与文化》2017 年 19 期）和讨论。

欧洲科学院院士、西班牙圣地亚哥联合大学让·莫内讲席教授、比较文学系教授塞萨尔·多明戈斯教授（Cesar Dominguez），及美国科学院院士、芝加哥大学比较文学教授苏源熙（Haun Saussy）等学者合著的比较文学专著（Introducing Comparative literature: New Trends and Applications[24]）高度评价了比较文学变异学。苏源熙引用了《比较文学变异学》（英文版）中的部分内容，阐明比较文学变异学是十分重要的成果。与比较文学法国学派和美国学派形成对比，曹顺庆教授倡导第三阶段理论，即，新奇的、科学的中国学派的模式，以及具有中国学派本身的研究方法的理论创新与中国学派"（《比较文学变异学》（英文版）第 43 页）。通过对"中西文化异质性的"跨文明研究"，曹顺庆教授的看法会更进一步的发展与进步（《比较文学变异学》（英文版）第 43 页），这对于中国文学理论的转化和西方文学理论的意义具有十分重要的价值。（"Another important contribution in the direction of an imparative comparative literature-at least as procedure-is Cao Shunqing's 2013 *The Variation Theory of Comparative Literature*. In contrast to the "French School" and "American School" of comparative Literature, Cao advocates a "third-phrase theory", namely, "a novel and scientific mode of the Chinese school," a "theoretical innovation and systematization of the Chinese school by relying on our *own* methods" (*Variation Theory* 43; emphasis added). From this etic beginning, his proposal moves forward emically by developing a "cross-civilizaional study on the heterogeneity between

---

24 Cesar Dominguez, Haun Saussy, Dario Villanueva Introducing Comparative literature: New Trends and Applications，Routledge, 2015

Chinese and Western culture" (43), which results in both the foreignization of Chinese literary theories and the Signification of Western literary theories.）

　　法国索邦大学（Sorbonne University）比较文学系主任伯纳德·弗朗科（Bernard Franco）教授在他出版的专著（《比较文学：历史、范畴与方法》）*La littératurecomparée: Histoire, domaines, méthodes* 中以专节引述变异学理论，他认为曹顺庆教授提出了区别于影响研究与平行研究的"第三条路"，即"变异理论"，这对应于观点的转变，从"跨文化研究"到"跨文明研究"。变异理论基于不同文明的文学体系相互碰撞为形式的交流过程中以产生新的文学元素，曹顺庆将其定义为"研究不同国家的文学现象所经历的变化"。因此曹顺庆教授提出的变异学理论概述了一个新的方向，并展示了比较文学在不同语言和文化领域之间建立多种可能的桥梁。（Il évoque l'hypothèse d'une troisième voie, la « théorie de la variation », qui correspond à un déplacement du point de vue, de celui des « études interculturelles » vers celui des « études transcivilisationnelles . » Cao Shunqing la définit comme « l'étude des variations subies par des phénomènes littéraires issus de différents pays, avec ou sans contact factuel, en même temps que l'étude comparative de l'hétérogénéité et de la variabilité de différentes expressions littéraires dans le même domaine ».Cette hypothèse esquisse une nouvelle orientation et montre la multiplicité des passerelles possibles que la littérature comparée établit entre domaines linguistiques et culturels différents.）[25]。

　　美国哈佛大学（Harvard University）厄内斯特·伯恩鲍姆讲席教授、比较文学教授大卫·达姆罗什（David Damrosch）对该专著尤为关注。他认为《比较文学变异学》（英文版）以中国视角呈现了比较文学学科话语的全球传播的有益尝试。曹顺庆教授对变异的关注提供了较为适用的视角，一方面超越了亨廷顿式简单的文化冲突模式，另一方面也跨越了同质性的普遍化。[26]国际学界对于变异学理论的关注已经逐渐从其创新性价值探讨延伸至文学研究，例如斯蒂文·托托西近日在 *Cultura* 发表的（Peripheralities: "Minor" Literatures, Women's Literature, and Adrienne Orosz de Csicser's Novels）一文中便成功地将变异学理论运用于阿德里安·奥罗兹的小说研究中。

25 Bernard Franco La littératurecomparée: Histoire, domaines, méthodes，Armand Colin 2016.
26 David Damrosch Comparing the Literatures,Literary Studies in a Global Age,Princeton University Press,2020.

　　国际学界对于比较文学变异学的认可也证实了变异学作为一种普遍性理论提出的初衷，其合法性与适用性将在不同文化的学者实践中巩固、拓展与深化。它不仅仅是跨文明研究的方法，而是一种具有超越影响研究和平行研究，超越西方视角或东方视角的宏大视野、一种建立在文化异质性和变异性基础之上的融汇创生、一种追求世界文学和总体问题最终理想的哲学关怀。

　　以如此篇幅展现中国比较文学之况，是因为中国比较文学研究本就是在各种危机论、唱衰论的压力下，各种质疑论、概念论中艰难前行，不探源溯流难以体察今日中国比较文学研究成果之不易。文明的多样性发展离不开文明之间的交流互鉴。最具"跨文明"特征的比较文学学科更需要文明之间成果的共享、共识、共析与共赏，这是我们致力于比较文学研究领域的学术理想。

　　千里之行，不积跬步无以至，江海之阔，不积细流无以成！如此宏大的一套比较文学研究丛书得承花木兰总编辑杜洁祥先生之宏志，以及该公司同仁之辛劳，中国比较文学学者之鼎力相助，才可顺利集结出版，在此我要衷心向诸君表达感谢！中国比较文学研究仍有一条长远之途需跋涉，期以系列丛书一展全貌，愿读者诸君敬赐高见！

曹顺庆

二零二一年十月二十三日于成都锦丽园

序：探梅踏雪几何时？

诗，可译，还是不可译？

——当然，不可译。

尤其中国古诗，精妙绝伦，叹为观止，英文，如何再现？

读遍中外译者各类译文，失望，总是难免的。

然而，诗歌翻译却一直在继续着，因为语言不通，诗歌需要交流。翻译，又是必然的。

尤其中国古典诗歌，在中国文化走出去的当下，急需走向英语世界。

大概二三百年来，从英国传教士到美国汉学家，再到中国学者，涌现了大批的古诗英译者。孰是？孰非？

有人说：外国译者不可信，对中国古诗理解和表达不到位；有人说：中国译者不可靠，对英文缺乏敏锐之感觉与把握。

我说：译者不在中外，在于译者的勤奋用功程度及其语言天赋之不同。语言天赋，盖天生而然，而译者的努力，却呈现主观之态。中国译者普遍存在的问题，我以为，就是英文阅读太少，英文借鉴太少——岂止中国译者？英美译者对英文的借鉴，固然有之，有时也对原文拘泥不化，英文表达平淡乏味，从而导致译诗不能出彩。译诗之乏力不逮，盖由此而生。

诗之为诗，或曰好诗，无非两端：一曰诗思巧妙，一曰语言巧妙。译诗之成败，实在关乎语言质量之高下优劣。因此，译诗好坏，不在译者之国籍，而在译者之英文阅读和英文修养。——不阅不读，胡瞻尔译有靓点兮？

　　《英文阅读与古诗英译》重在启发译者阅读广泛英文，以期提高译诗质量。

　　宋人辛弃疾《一剪梅·游蒋山呈叶丞相》写得甚好：

　　　　独立苍茫醉不归。日暮天寒，归去来兮。探梅踏雪几何时？今
　　我来思，杨柳依依。

　　　　白石冈头曲岸西。一片闲愁，芳草萋萋。多情山鸟不须啼。桃
　　李无言，下自成蹊。

　　日夜沉浸于英文阅读和古诗英译之中，我只觉得辛弃疾抒发的，正是译诗之情：

　　　　我独自徘徊于汉英诗歌之间，境界阔大无边，如饮甘露，如品
　　美酒，陶醉于语言之美，忘记把家还。日已暮，天正寒，归去，归
　　去！无边景，雪中情，探梅寻春雪中行，如何传诗情？诗思恰如梦，
　　杨柳依依满含情。长江西岸，白石岗，萋萋草正芳。常念古诗难译
　　好，闲愁了未了。我思我想我缱绻，山鸟啼叫欢。妖艳桃李无需言，
　　引众人来攀，留下脚印一串串。——怪来诗思清入骨，门对寒流雪
　　满山。

　　诗，可译，还是不可译？

　　即便可译，也是难上加难。宋人杨万里《过松源晨炊漆公店》，又写到了古诗英译之难：

　　　　莫言下岭便无难，赚得行人空喜欢。

　　　　正入万山圈子里，一山放出一山拦。

　　是的，古诗英译，正是雪中情，山中行。

　　清代才子纳兰性德，用其诗句鼓励着译者："山一程，水一程，身向榆关那畔行，夜深千帐灯。"

张智中　2022 年 9 月 25 日　松间居

目

次

理论篇

一、英文阅读与古诗英译

　　如果我们抛开诗歌的众多因素不予考虑，只看译诗语言的话，就会发现绝大部分中国译者译诗的语言，非常单调贫乏，有时连散文的语言都远远没有达到，更遑论诗歌。英译汉，需要译者很好的汉语修养；汉译英，则需要译者良好的英文修养。一个好的英译汉的译者，会一辈子坚持学习来提高自己的中文，一个好的汉译英的译者，同样会终生阅读英文，以保持其英文的鲜活地道。

　　在这一方面，美国著名翻译家葛浩文（Howard Goldblatt）是我们学习的榜样。"他认为，他的很多同仁译家花费大量时间研读汉语，以至于丧失了对英语的感觉，翻译时过于受原文束缚，往往使译文大失文采。他一直保持阅读优秀英文作品的习惯，以使自己的英文跟得上时代的发展。他呼吁翻译同行多读优秀英文作品，培养英语语感。"[1]

　　其实，葛浩文在多个场合，都反复强调英文阅读的重要性。当被问及觉得译者素养是怎样养成的？葛浩文说："多看，多看一些英文的，多看一些小说，多看一些翻译的，翻成英文的，德国的，北欧的，不管是哪国的，我都要看。"[2]又问：为什么要看翻译的呢？葛浩文说："这些也要是以英文为主的，我要看

1　吕敏宏，论葛浩文中国现当代小说译介［A］，刘云虹，葛浩文翻译研究［C］，南京：南京大学出版社，2019：47。

2　闫怡恂、葛浩文，文学翻译：过程与标准——葛浩文访谈录［A］，刘云虹，葛浩文翻译研究［C］，南京：南京大学出版社，2019：667。

他怎么处理。当然英文原作看得最多。"³

总之，葛浩文强调翻译的杂读，以阅读英文原著为主，兼顾各种好的翻译的阅读，对一个译者是非常重要的。因此，美国俄克拉荷马大学的中文教授Jonathan Stalling 认为，"葛浩文的译文跟莫言的原文旗鼓相当，是莫言小说在英语中的回声，是英语所能允许的臻于极致的回声。"⁴

反观国内译者，"很多中国译者的汉译英作品，每一句话都是漂亮的英文，挑不出任何语法错误，逻辑严密，条理清晰，但是读来就是呆板，没味道。其中一个原因就是不够习俗化，没有时代感。"⁵说得直率一些，中国译者的阅读太少，尤其是英文阅读，少得可怜，甚至不具备熟练的高级英文阅读的能力，就开始做汉译英，甚至汉诗英译，从而导致译文的失败。国内可能有读者喜欢，但英语读者却不买账。

葛浩文说："读英文小说首先是因为我喜欢读，是一种消遣。更重要的是，阅读别人用英文创作的小说，看他们如何遣词造句，我也能从中学习。看书的时候我手边总是放着纸笔，读到什么有趣的东西就会马上记下来。……坦白说，很多做翻译的人英文书籍读得不够。母语是英语的译者花很多时间读汉语，这当然很可取，但他们的英语水平却停滞了，不能持续地增加英文表达能力，所以我总是对想做汉译英的人说，要多读些英语书籍。汉语要读，但更要读英语，这样才会了解现在的美国和英国的日常语言是怎样的。"⁶葛浩文所强调的，是语言式的阅读。其实，大凡著名的翻译家，没有一个不是阅读的痴迷者。刘士聪也反复强调英文阅读的重要性，嘱咐学生每天坚持英文阅读，品味措词用语之妙。因此，他的汉译英才地道可读。杨宪益在中学时期，就是阅读狂人，每天坚持一两本英文原著的阅读，到后来自己的英文跟自己的中文，几乎是一样的程度了，所以才取得了"翻译了大半个中国"的辉煌成就。

---

3 闫怡恂、葛浩文，文学翻译：过程与标准——葛浩文访谈录［A］，刘云虹，葛浩文翻译研究［C］，南京：南京大学出版社，2019：667。

4 孙会军，葛浩文和他的中国文学译介［M］，上海：上海交通大学出版社，2016：174。

5 吕敏宏，论葛浩文中国现当代小说译介［A］，刘云虹，葛浩文翻译研究［C］，南京：南京大学出版社，2019：48。

6 李文静，中国文学英译的合作、协商与文化传播——汉英翻译家葛浩文与林丽君访谈录［A］，刘云虹，葛浩文翻译研究［C］，南京：南京大学出版社，2019：620。

二、读者定位与译者的英文阅读

汉诗英译的终极读者，当为英美人士，那么，翻译策略便处处为其考虑。"好的翻译不译字，不译句，译的是意，是味，是交际功能。是把读透的原文用译语重新写一遍。译就是写，是对原文的积极主动的重写（an active form of writing）。我们看到，不同的译者为不同的翻译目的或翻译不同类型的语篇的时候，重写的程度是不一样的。重写力度大的，删减、重组段落，甚至改动内容和情节的情况较为频繁，力度小的与原文在形式上更贴近些，但也必定是一种重写。原文的表层形式要保留（因为形式是有意义的），但译者必须摆脱其形式上的束缚，积极主动地发挥自己的写作能力，把原文重写好。"[7]李运兴所言极是。他又说："想做好翻译，我们首先要自问的，不是我有没有翻译技巧，而是我的源语理解如何，译语写作能力如何。翻译技巧是什么？是教师、学者们从好的译作中总结出来的、带有规律性的原则和方法。但这些方法只是无法独立存在的毛，必须依附在语言功力这张皮上。没有语言功力，技巧的作用无从发挥。就汉译英而言，英语写作能力有了，翻译中表达阶段的难题就有了解决的基础。"[8]

是的，就汉诗英译而言，考验译者水平或能力的，其实就是其英语写作的能力。想要提高我们的英语写作能力，就必读坚持英文阅读，并悉心体会，善加利用。作为汉诗英译的结果的译诗，应该像英诗，甚至像一流的英美诗人写出来的英语诗歌，才能吸引英美读者；译诗有了真正意义上的英美读者，才是我们译诗的真正成功。

文学翻译或汉诗英译，是一种欣赏和再创作的艺术审美体验。"一个翻译家，不管他的翻译思想和艺术才能如何，最终都要在驾驭目的语的表达力上受到严格的考验。"[9]但是，"笔者在翻译诗学研究过程中发现一个不可绕过的话题被翻译界疏忽了，那就是译者的基本能力或翻译能力的核心问题：双语语感能力。进而笔者又发现，译者还有一个对诗的感觉的问题，也就是更高层次的语感问题，译者是否具备双语诗感（诗歌修养）能力。这些最为核心的问题也

---

7 李运兴，前言［A］，李运兴，英译中国名家散文选：汉英对照［Z］，上海：上海外语教育出版社，2019。

8 李运兴，前言［A］，李运兴，英译中国名家散文选：汉英对照［Z］，上海：上海外语教育出版社，2019。

9 黎昌抱，王佐良翻译风格研究［M］，北京：光明日报出版社，2009：10。

被理论界忽视了。"[10]

因此，提倡以汉诗英译为导向的英文阅读，其重要性再强调也不过分。只有坚持以汉诗英译为导向的英文阅读，才能切实地提高译者的诗感，才能提高汉诗英译的质量。"语感至少有三个层次：一个是属于本能的母语语感（intuition），这是自然而然生成的；二是二语语感（sense），可以靠知识体系构建，可以培养而成；第三个是诗感，对语言美的感念（feeling）。诗感是语感的最高层次，诗感相当于人对艺术美的感觉，换句话说就是个体在语言艺术上的最高鉴赏力。"[11]很多中国学者和外国学者，都强调翻译过程中阅读的重要性。爱尔兰翻译理论家迈克尔克罗宁（Cronin）提出："强调阅读是一个特别有难度的领域，而且把阅读课作为翻译课程的一部分，是非常有效的做法。……翻译教师的任务就是如何把大量的阅读作为唯一的主导模式，以期达到提高学生的整体人文素养和文本写作能力的效果。"[12]

阅读是学习和提高翻译能力的前提和基础。其实，阅读的目的分为多种，其中一种，可谓为翻译的阅读，为汉译英的阅读，或者为汉诗英译的阅读。我们在阅读英文的过程中，脑子里想着汉语诗歌，一旦有了联想，就随时记录，并善加运用。这种带着翻译意识的阅读，或为了汉诗英译的阅读，是一种逆向思维的阅读。最好的汉译英，是英文译成汉语之后，把汉语当做原文之后相应的"原文"。这样的"原文"，当然是真正的原汁原味的原文。因此，这是最为有效的阅读。

要想翻译出高质量、高水平的译文，就必须有目的地进行大量的阅读。翻译是语言的输出，而阅读是语言的输入。没有输入，则没有输出。因此，对于译者而言，阅读的重要性，再强调也不过分。互文阅读强化了对原文的阐释，并使译文的产出富于理据。因此，译者要根据翻译情境，制定相应的互文阅读策略。只有经过这种大量带着翻译意识的阅读，才能有效提高翻译能力，提高译文的质量。从互文性角度来看，经典英文阅读在语言水平、文化知识、语篇形式、译者主体性四个层面，对汉诗英译起到积极的作用。因此，加强译者的互文性阅读，是提高汉诗英译水平的一条切实有效的途径。

诗歌的魅力，在很大程度上，至少在一定程度上，来自诗歌的语言魅力。

---

10 汤富华，翻译的诗学批评［M］，南京：南京大学出版社，2019：215-216。
11 汤富华，翻译的诗学批评［M］，南京：南京大学出版社，2019：22。
12 陶友兰、强晓，本科翻译专业阅读教学综合模式探讨［J］，中国翻译，2015，(1)。

诗歌，说到底，就是语言的艺术。诗人兼评论家马修·阿诺德（Mattew Arnold）说："诗歌简直就是最完美、最深刻、最有效的言说事物的方式。（Poetry is simply the most beautiful, the most impressive, and the most effective mode of saying things.）"[13]是的，"在诗歌的艺术领域里，对语言的修炼和构思方面的技巧是无穷无尽的。而通过诗歌，我们才更加看到了语言本身丰富多彩、变换无穷的魅力。"[14]是的，"诗歌语言的特殊之处，在于它被诗人使用和言说的方式。"[15]一些普通的词语，在特定的语境下，可以产生诗意的联想，不仅在诗歌中，在散文中，也是如此。因此，散文中的语言，可以用于诗歌；英文散文或英文小说中的一些语言，也可用于汉诗英译，而不仅限于英文诗歌。

三、古诗英译的语言策略

英文语言表达的发展，整体上呈弃繁从简的趋势。我们提倡以汉诗英译为目的互文性阅读，目的就是吸取当代英文之精华，用活泼、清新、凝练、诗意的当代英文，来传达中国古代诗歌之意境。林语堂曾感叹："夫译难事，译中国古文为今日英文则尤难"。[16]虽然林语堂说的是古文英译，但把中国古诗翻译成当代清新可读的英文，有同样的难度。就汉诗英译或古诗英译而言，如果我们只是追求字意、句意正确，以及押韵格律的完美，这是远远不够的。文学翻译，非文字翻译；古诗英译，不是译韵，而是译诗，关键在于译诗语言的运筹和意境的再造上。只有这样，才能切实地提高汉诗英译的水平和质量，引无数西方读者为中国古诗之魅力竞折腰。

"中国经典文化的对外传播状况一直不理想，中国的圣贤从未像苏格拉底、柏拉图、亚里士多德影响中国一样影响西方。尽管从利马窦开始，就不断有汉学家将中国经典著作译成外文，从清末至今，也有不少中国翻译家从事中国典籍外译，但这些译著都只是对国外汉学界比较有影响，其他民众，包括一般的知识分子，对中华文化经典仍然陌生。"[17]又，"与托尔斯泰、巴尔扎克、

13　黄遵洸，英诗咀华［M］，杭州：浙江工商大学出版社，2014：4。

14　沈庆利，写在心灵边上：中外抒情诗歌欣赏［M］，北京：中国纺织出版社，2001：173。

15　黄遵洸，英诗咀华［M］，杭州：浙江工商大学出版社，2014：13。

16　吴慧坚，林语堂译介实践的当代诠释与经验借鉴——以《孔子的智慧》为例［A］，陈煜斓，语堂智慧　智慧语堂［C］，福州：福建教育出版社，2016：284。

17　吴慧坚，林语堂译介实践的当代诠释与经验借鉴——以《孔子的智慧》为例［A］，陈煜斓，语堂智慧　智慧语堂［C］，福州：福建教育出版社，2016：274。

安徒生等在国内的认知程度相比，国外又有多少读者知道李白、杜甫、白居易？"[18]原因何在呢？"比如翻译作品，我们以前常常以为某部经典作品好，就理所当然地以为外国读者也一定会认可其'好'，于是花费大量人力物力孜孜不倦地翻译出来了，也'送出去'了，结果因为不了解国外读者的阅读习惯，以及其当代的语言表达习惯，外国人只能像我们读中国古文一样去读我们送出去的中国作品。"[19]

是的，"国外读者的阅读习惯，以及其当代的语言表达习惯"——就古诗英译而言，这个东西无疑被忽略了，尤其对中国译者而言。古诗英译需要在西方英语国家打开市场，其读者不应该仅限于国外的汉学界，这就要求我们努力做到"中国立场，国际表达"。具体说来，"针对不同读者的需求，可采取两种基本策略：一是学术性翻译，其读者对象是潜心研究传统中国文化的专家学者；译者在翻译时需细读原文，解释典故，考释出处。这种翻译突出的是译文的研究价值和文化价值。另一种翻译方法是普及性翻译，面对普通读者大众，注重文笔的生动传神，注重可读性、大众化。前者可以采取适当异化的翻译策略，后者可以采取适当归化的翻译策略。"[20]

中国文化走出去，中国诗歌走出去，我们心目当中的读者，就不应该是仅仅是外国汉学界的专家和学者，更应该是英美国家的文学爱好者或普通大众。那么，采取译诗语言的归化策略，就显得非常重要。我们所倡导的读英文译古诗，或者朝向古诗英译的英文阅读，就是保证译文语言归化地道的一个重要措施。至于讨论多时而没有结论的问题，例如古诗英译的理想译者，到底是中国译者还是外国译者？我们认为当然是中国译者——只是，中国译者要做的事情还很多，还有很长的路要走。"在原文的准确理解方面，充分发挥国内译者的优势，而在译文的表达和可接受度方面，充分发挥国外母语译者的优势。"[21]"发挥国外母语译者的优势"，我们认为，不是跟外国译者合作，而是中国译者大量阅读，特别是进行朝向汉诗英译的英文阅读和积累。

18 孙宜学，中华文化国际传播：途径与方法创新［M］，上海：同济大学出版社，2016：127。

19 孙宜学，中华文化国际传播：途径与方法创新［M］，上海：同济大学出版社，2016：127。

20 王宏，基于"大中华文库"的中国典籍英译翻译策略研究［M］，杭州：浙江大学出版社，2019：465。

21 王宏，基于"大中华文库"的中国典籍英译翻译策略研究［M］，杭州：浙江大学出版社，2019：465。

同时，我们也应该清醒地看到，中国译者取得成功的案例，相对较少；西方读者所喜欢读的古诗英译，自韦利和庞德以来，基本上都是出自西方译者的手笔。这一现象，更值得我们反思。不过，"由中国译者主导和参与的中国典籍英译历史不长，仍处于实验性探索阶段。唯有依靠多种翻译渠道，采取多种翻译模式、翻译手段和翻译策略，循序渐进，多管齐下，中国典籍英译才能日趋成熟，走向繁荣。"[22]

中国古诗词为什么不能翻译？因为古诗词是由能指所催生的一种诗，是形式决定内容的，形式发生在内容之前，形式变化了，诗意基本也没了。这不是翻译水准高低的问题，不论你水准高低，在你一提笔翻译的刹那，便已经错了。古诗词不但不能翻译成外文，连翻译成现代白话诗也不行，因为就古诗词的所指而言，大部分就是一篇散文，既便在翻译中有效保留了所指，也只是保留了一小段散文而已，是没有诗意的，甚至是无意义的。

因此，阅读英文并汲取英文之精华，在古诗英译中就显得尤其重要。我们相信，只要中国译者坚持读英文译古诗，坚持不断的阅读和积累，并善加运用，我们就可以译出中国古典诗歌的优秀译文，让中国古典诗歌在当前的国际语境下，发出独特的光芒和魅力。

四、读英文，译古诗

读英文，译古诗，是我们的翻译理念。作为译者，我们必须顾及英语语言的表达习惯，那么，就必须坚持阅读英文，而且要大量阅读。"因袭性给汉译英学习的最大启迪就是，必须把英语原创语篇阅读作为战略选择，持之以恒。"[23]如果找到与汉语古典诗词类似的英文表达，就应该运用到译文中，以便增强译文的英文效果。相反，"如果依然照搬汉语的语言表达形式，则很难符合英语语言的表达习惯和特点，从而很难使译文在译入语国家的读者群中产生共鸣，影响翻译目标的实现。"[24]英译中国的小说、散文、诗歌，都是一样的道理。

---

22 王宏，基于"大中华文库"的中国典籍英译翻译策略研究［M］，杭州：浙江大学出版社，2019：466。

23 李运兴，前言［A］，李运兴，英译中国名家散文选：汉英对照［Z］，上海：上海外语教育出版社，2019。

24 束慧娟，基于意义进化论的典籍英译模式研究［M］，苏州：苏州大学出版社，2019：111。

中国译者的古诗英译之所以没有吸引西方读者，主要因为语言贫乏，缺乏文采，或曰缺乏英文之借鉴与创新使用。纵观 20 世纪 80 年代或者更早时期以来的古诗英译，早期译者的成就，似乎不比当下译者的成就差，因为他们更注重英文的修养。因此，译文常有亮点。例如杜甫《春望》及其英译：

春望	**A View in Spring**
国破山河在，	Hill and valley survive a country broken,
城春草木深。	Grass and trees grow deep in a town in Spring.
感时花溅泪，	Affected by events the flowers shed tears;
恨别鸟惊心。	Who mourn separation start to hear birds sing,
烽火连三月，	Beacons have flamed for three months running, hence
家书抵万金。	Letters from home are worth their weight in gold.
白头搔更短，	A white head scratched its hairs grow less
浑欲不胜簪。	Till hairpins simply lose their hold.
	（谢文通　译）

译诗采取格律体，但却较少油滑的味道。译文中，Beacons have flamed，three months running，worth their weight in gold，hairpins simply lose their hold 等，都是非常地道而新颖有力的英文表达。

杜甫的《春夜喜雨》及其英译：

春夜喜雨	**Rejoicing in Rain on a Spring Night**
好雨知时节，	The good rain knows its season when to fall
当春乃发生。	As it does whenever Spring comes round:
随风潜入夜，	Stealing into the night behind the wind
润物细无声。	To moisten all things fine without a sound.
野径云俱黑，	On country paths the clouds are a dark pall
江船火独明。	The river boats pinpoint with light for a foil.
晓看红湿处，	At dawn we see on the trail of sodden pink
花重锦官城。	The flowers hang heavy from the city wall.
	（谢文通　译）

将"野径云俱黑"译为 the clouds are a dark pall（云彩是黑色的棺罩），运用暗喻，形象贴切。"江船火独明"译为 The river boats pinpoint with light for a foil（江上的船只，有了光线的衬托，可以精确找到。）其中，动词 pinpoint，意为"精确地找到；瞄准"。例如：

It's difficult to pinpoint the cause of the accident.

很难清楚地找到事故发生的原因。

With this device, we can pinpoint your exact location.

有了这个仪器，我们可以精确地标出你的位置。

名词 foil，意为"箔；陪衬物；陪衬者"。

另外，倒数第三行的 the trail of sodden pink（湿透的粉红色的小径），其中形容词 sodden 与名词 pink 的搭配，也令人感到新颖。

总之，译诗几处亮点，可见译者精湛的英文功力。

杜甫《春夜喜雨》笔者原来的英译：

A Joyous Rain in Spring Night　Du Fu

A good rain knows the best season

Is the advent of spring. With wind

It steals into the night, to moisten

Myriads of things silently.

Murky clouds over dark field path;

A fishing boat is solitarily twinkling.

The dawn sees wet flowers which

Dot and decorate the Silk Town.

晨读英文，读到这样一个句子：

The chills of long winter had suddenly given way; the north wind has spent its last gasp; and a mild air came stealing from the west, breathing the breath of life into nature, and wooing every bud and flower to burst forth into fragrance and beauty.

于是想起《春夜喜雨》的英译：数年前的译作，现在读来，似觉死板。受 Washington Irving 英文句子的启发，对原诗融会贯通，综合掂量，改译如下，首先散体：

A Joyous Rain in Spring Night　Du Fu

A timely rain comes stealing against a gentle wind in the depth of the night of an early spring, moistening myriads of things silently. Murky clouds over dark field path; a fishing boat is solitarily twinkling. The dawn sees clusters of dewy flowers, which dot and decorate the Silk Town.

诗体排列：

A Joyous Rain in Spring Night　Du Fu
A timely rain comes stealing against
a gentle wind in the depth of the night
of an early spring, moistening myriads
of things silently. Murky clouds over
dark field path; a fishing boat is
solitarily twinkling. The dawn
sees clusters of dewy flowers,
which dot and decorate
the Silk Town.

再看一首：

绝句四首（三）	**The Third of Four Quatrains**
两个黄鹂鸣翠柳， 一行白鹭上青天。 窗含西岭千秋雪， 门泊东吴万里船。	Two orioles sing within the willows' green, A line of white herons fly into the blue. My windows frame the snow of ages on West Range, At my door is moored the thousand-league-boat to Jiangsu.[25] （谢文通　译）

译诗首行，把 green 用作名词，within 与 willows 形成头韵，颇有诗意；第二行中，the blue 与 green 形成对照。第三行中，动词 frame 形象，有不少其他译者也采用此词；the snow of ages 措语地道。如果说译诗少有不足的话，该是最后的专名 Jiangsu：一方面，唐代没有当今江苏的概念；另一方面，西方读者怎么知道 Jiangsu 是哪里呢？究其原因，还是为了让 Jiangsu 与第二行尾的 blue 押韵。

不过，总体说来，谢文通的译诗，体现了译者很好的英文功底和翻译水平。谢文通何人？据网上资料：谢文通，1909 年 4 月出生，1930 年获燕京大学政治学学士学位，1933 年获美国加利福尼亚大学文学硕士学位。归国后，他先后在西北联合大学外国语言文学系、西南联合大学外国语言文学系、浙江大学外国语言文学系、北京大学外国语言文学系和中山大学外语系工作。谢文通研究成果丰硕，1959 年在商务印书馆出版了著作《英语文学文选》，1979 年在

---

25 谢文通，杜诗选译［Z］，广州：广东高等教育出版社，1985：327。

《现代外语》上发表论文《杜诗英译数首》，此外他还在国外期刊上发表多篇论文。

之所以引用他的几首译诗，是因为在中国翻译界或诗歌翻译界，谢文通几乎被人遗忘了。而他的译诗却语言地道，甚至不乏亮点，是个不应被忽略的译者。其他如翁显良、徐忠杰等老一辈译者，常见有人研究，当然，更不用说许渊冲、汪榕培等翻译名家了。总之，我们不仅要读英文，不仅要学习西方译者，也要学习中国译者，特别是老一代译者身上的优点，包括那些几乎被人遗忘的译者。

五、英译汉：同词异译的启发——以 warm, faint, gather 为例

不仅是汉诗英译，即便在散文的汉译英里，也需要英文语言的变化多姿，这样译文才能出彩。比如不同语境下的同词异译：在一个较大或较长的语篇中，如果只是同词同译，译文会显得干瘪乏味；若能花样翻新，则会多一些美学效果。

首先，从英译汉的角度而言，来看几个相同英文单词的不同汉译。下面含 warm 的句子，我们观察其对应的汉语译文：

英语原文	汉　译
The day had been **warm** and sunny; and, in the cool of the evening, the whole family went out to drive.	这天天气**暖**和，阳光明媚；晚上凉爽时全家坐车出去兜风。
I was really in love, I felt a **warmth** at my heart which glowed in my face.	我真的坠入了爱河，我感觉心头发**热**，脸上发光。
Being in bed with your lover is a fine thing, but returning to her in its night-long **warmth** is sweet.	与情人同床共枕是一大快事，而重回她的身旁，沐浴在一夜余**温**中，实乃甜蜜无比。
One of the windows in the living room was open, and the fragrance of flowers baked by the sun was thick enough to stuff one's nose and **warm** enough to make one drowsy.	客堂一扇窗开着，太阳烘焙的花香，浓得塞鼻子，**暖**得使人头脑迷倦。
He went to one of the windows and threw open the shutter. A flood of **warm** light streamed into the room.	他走到一扇窗户前拉起了百叶窗，一大片阳光流泻到屋里来。

在以上例子中，warm 或其变形是"温暖"的本意；下面例子中，warm 或

其变形则是"温暖"的引申义。

I have a **warm** heart and a vivacious fancy.	我有一颗热切的心和丰富的想象力。
I felt a **warm** glow of satisfaction.	我感到了一种极大的满足。
Her eyes were **warm** with smiles as she gave him his tea.	她递茶给他，眼里是暖暖的笑意。
Keep **warm** old man.	别泄气，老伯。
If he had not said charming things to her his eyes, **warm** with admiration, would have betrayed him. His ease was delightful.	虽然他嘴上没有对她说出迷人的话语，可是，那双含有炽热爱慕的眼睛却出卖了他。他的轻松自在惹人喜爱。
She flushed up **warmly** and whispered back.	她红着脸轻轻的回答。
…, which meant she was not a Chinese citizen, so they did not quite **warm** up to her.	……，算不得中国国籍，不大去亲近她。
Miss Liu was the last to arrive. She had a **warm** frank-looking face and an ample figure. Her clothes were quite tight so that creases appeared at her slightest movement.	刘小姐最后一个到。坦白可亲的脸，身体很丰满，衣服颇紧，一动衣服上就起波纹。
He was immediately shown in by his father-in-law, met Mr.Wang, and had a **warm** talk with him.	立刻由丈人陪了进去，见到王先生，谈得很投机。

下面句子中，都含有 faint 及其变形：

Her **faint** smile was like an overcast sky on a cold dreary day.	她冷淡的笑容，像阴寒欲雪天的淡日。
I was just in time to catch her as she fell forward in a **faint**.	她向前晕倒过去，我及时地扶住了她。
… and hunger has made him **faint**.	饥饿又使他差点昏厥。
… a fearful peal of thunder made them all start to their feet, and Mrs. Umney **fainted**.	一阵吓人的雷声使他们全都跳起来，厄姆尼太太晕了过去。
… the **faint** smile that just played across the lips was far too subtle to be really sweet.	那抹划过嘴唇的淡淡微笑，因为太微妙，所以算不上可爱。
He rose from his seat with a **faint** cry of joy.	他发出一声微弱的欢呼，从座位上站起来。
… said Birkin, a **faint** smile on his face.	说着脸上掠过一丝笑。
The swans had gone out on to the opposite bank, the reeds smelled sweet, a **faint** breeze touched the skin.	天鹅上了对岸，芦苇散发着清香，微风轻拂着人们的皮肤。

She realized that it was **faintly** moonlight.	她知道那是淡淡的月光。
Gerald listened with a **faint**, fine smile on his face.	杰拉德脸上挂着漂亮的微笑一直在听伯金说话。
The **faint** voice filtered to extinction.	那微弱的声音消逝了。
Faintly, the trees showed, like shadows. Then a house, white, had a curious distinctness.	树木渐渐显形了，像影子一般，然后是一间白房子，清楚得莫名其妙。
The English visitors could hear the occasional twanging of a zither, the strumming of a piano, snatches of laughter and shouting and singing, a **faint** vibration of voices.	英国人听得到偶然传来的奇特琴声、漫不经心敲出来的钢琴声和说笑、喊叫及歌声，不过听不大清。

下面句子中，都含有 gather 及其变形：

He **gathered** his thoughts and walked over to a policeman behind a desk.	他整理了一下自己的思绪，向桌子后面的警察走去。
Van Helsing seemed surprised, and his brows **gathered** as if in thought, but he said nothing.	范海星看起来很吃惊，他的眉毛拧到了一起，仿佛在思考，但是什么也没说。
It was strange to see the snow falling in such heavy flakes close to us, and beyond, the sun shining more and more brightly as it sank down towards the far mountain tops. Sweeping the glass all around us I could see here and there dots moving singly and in twos and threes and larger numbers - the wolves were **gathering** for their prey.	很奇怪，我们眼前的雪下得很大，但是在它们的外面太阳越来越明亮，向远处的山顶望去，我能看见到处都有移动着的圆点，一个，两个，三个，越来越多。狼群正在向它们的猎物包围过来。
All around, shadow was **gathering** from the trees.	四下里树林的阴影开始变得浓重起来。
As the day wore on, the life-blood seemed to ebb away from Ursula, and within the emptiness a heavy despair **gathered**. Her passion seemed to bleed to death, and there was nothing. She sat suspended in a state of complete nullity, harder to bear than death.	一天渐渐过去，厄秀拉变得不那么有生气了，她感到极端空虚失望。她的激情之血快流干了。她陷入了上不着天下不着地的虚无中，这比死都难受。
Still he **didn't gather** enough resolution to move.	可他又没勇气一走了之。
…. he gradually **gathered** the whole situation into his mind.	……。对矿区的全部局势胸有成竹了。
Birkin sighed, and **gathered** his brows into a knot of anger.	伯金叹口气，生气地皱起眉头。

But he felt something icy **gathering** at his heart.	可是他感到心头愈来愈发凉。
She paused to **gather** up her thread again.	她停了停，理清了思绪。
He hesitated for a moment. Then he **gathered** himself together for a leap, to overtake her.	他犹豫了片刻，然后使尽全身力气跳起来去追她。

　　上面含有 warm，faint 或 gather 的句子，相应的汉语译文，却变化多姿。如果我们逆向思维，从汉译英的角度来看，这些汉语词语，大多都不对应英文单词的。而这样的英语"译文"，却是最为理想的"译文"。

六、汉译英：同词异译的启发——以"爱好""喜欢""由于" "总之"为例

　　就汉译英而言，例如下列句子中"爱好"的英译：英译一都千篇一律地把"爱好"译为 love，虽可达意，却显单调。英译二根据具体的语境和"爱好"的具体含义，选用不同的英语表达方式，或是单词，或是短语，译文便显得摇曳多姿、富于文采。

汉语原文	英译一	英译二
他对摄影有强烈的**爱好**。	He **loves** photography very much.	He **has a passion for** photography.
他生性**爱好**艺术。	He **loves** art by nature.	He **has a bent for** art.
摄影是他的**爱好**之一。	Photography is one of the things that he **loves**.	Photography is one of his **hobbies**.
他的**爱好**从下国际象棋到划独木舟，范围很广。	He **loves** many things, ranging from chess to canoeing.	His **interests** ranged from chess to canoeing.

　　来看"喜欢"的不同英译：

汉语原文	英　译
你喜欢学校生活吗？	Do you **like** campus life?
他们喜欢来自东方的绘画。	They **love** paintings from the Orient.
我最喜欢的是绘画。	What I most **enjoy** is painting.
他非常喜欢爬山。	He **is** very **fond of** mountaineering.
你喜欢做什么就做什么。	Do whatever you **please**.
钓鱼是他最喜欢的消遣。	Fishing is his **favorite** pursuit.

我非常喜欢英语。	I'm **crazy** about English.
我非常喜欢巧克力。	I **adore** chocolate.
她特别喜欢小马。	She has a **mania** for ponies.
我喜欢上热狗了。	I have **taken a fancy on** hot dog.
对于喜欢文化艺术的人来说，北京是座很吸引人的城市。	Beijing is a good city for anyone who **is interested in** culture.
我喜欢物理。	Physics is my **dish**.
我喜欢物理甚于化学。	I **prefer** physics **to** chemistry.
他生性不喜欢运动。	He has a temperamental **dislike** of sports.
他不喜欢人家取笑他的秃头。	He **hates** to be teased about his balding head.
我不喜欢抽烟。	Smoking is **distasteful** to me.
不知什么原因，我近来不喜欢吃鸡蛋。	I seem to have **gone off** eggs lately for some reason.
他花钱大手大脚且喜欢摆阔。	He is lavish and ostentatious.

如果说以上众多的"喜欢"或"不喜欢"，均有英译的话，最后一个句子里的"喜欢"，却不见英译的痕迹。但仔细品味，其意已包涵在 lavish 与 ostentatious 两个形容词里面了。

再来看"由于"的不同英译：

由于桥断了，得绕一段路。	There is a detour **because** the bridge is broken.
由于他的参与，我们赢了比赛。	We win the game **because of** his participation.
由于投资少，我们的工业生产一直停滞不前。	**Due to** low investment, our industrial output has remained stagnant.
由于我们的共同努力，任务提前完成了。	**Owing to** our joint efforts, the task was fulfilled ahead of schedule.
由于他的努力，获得了比我们预期的更大的成功。	**Thanks to** his effort, it is more successful than we have expected.
由于我们的合同快到期了，我们必须谈判新的合约。	**Since** our contract is near its term we must negotiate a new one.
由于时间仓促，记者们往往很少有机会能按照自己爱好的风格写稿。	**As a result of** the haste, reporters frequently have little opportunity to indulge in their own stylistic preferences.
他们的成功大半是由于作了充分的准备。	Their success was in great measure **the result of** thorough preparation.

由于坚持不懈的努力，他获得了学业上的成功。	He succeeded in his studies **by dint of** steadfast application.
许多物种由于人们的极端无知而灭绝了。	Many species have been wiped out **through** sublime ignorance.
他由于英勇而获得一枚奖章。	He received a medal **for** his heroism.
对由于我的疏忽而引起麻烦，非常抱歉。	I am sorry for all the trouble aroused **by** my negligence.
这架电视机由于使用太不小心而损坏了。	The TV set was damaged **from** rough usage.
他面部的毁损是由于一次爆炸造成的。	The disfigurement of his face **was caused by** an explosion.
他说他们公司之所以获得成功是由于全体员工的团结和坚持不懈努力工作的结果。	He **attributed** his company's success **to** the unity of all the staff and their persevering hard work.
出席率低是由于天气不佳。	The bad weather **is responsible for** the small attendance.
他的错误是由于粗枝大叶而造成的。	His error **stemmed from** carelessness.
他工作中的困难是由于缺乏经验而引起的。	His difficulties in his work **issue from** his lack of experience.
他的病是由于吃了变质的食物所致。	His illness **resulted from** bad food.
由于暴雪，加上我伤风，我无法去拜访他。	I couldn't visit him, **what with** the snowstorm and the cold I had.
由于此人的罪名在法庭上未能证实，所以未被判刑。	The man went scot-free **when** the charges against him couldn't be proved in court.
由于没有提前通知我们要来吃晚饭，我们只能吃些家常便饭。	Having arrived unannounced for supper, we had to take potluck.
由于时间不够，现在不能深入讨论这个问题。	Lack of time forbids any further discussion at the point.
由于电力不足，街道昏暗。	The shortage of power dimmed the streets.
她由于羞怯，未曾向他吐露真情实意。	Her modesty prevented her from making her real feelings known to him.

　　在上引最后四个译例中，英文不见"由于"的痕迹，但已转化为现在分词短语或名词短语了。根据"由于"的具体含义和具体语境，选用不同的英语表达方式，或是单词，或是短语，或者对语序句法重新组合安排，从而使得译文更加地道。特别是在同一个语境内，若只会用 because 来对译"因为"，则语言何其单调贫乏。只有善于变化，才能使增进译文的风姿。

最后，来看"总之"的不同英译：

总之，我们应该改进我们的服务。	**In a word**, then, we should improve our service.
总之，你做得不好。	**In brief,** your work is bad.
总之，谣言不可信。	The rumor, **in short**, is not to be trusted.
总之，计划告吹了。	**In sum**, the plan failed.
总之，那两所大学有一些共同之处。	**In summary** the two universities have some things in common.
总之，这是故事很恰当的结尾。	It was, **in fine**, a fitting end to the story.
总之，项目会受到影响。	**In any case**, the project suffers.
总之，成功来自于努力。	**To sum up**, success results from hard work.
总之，不对称是非常明显的。	**In any event** the asymmetry is clear enough.
总之，我身体非常好。	**In other words**, I'm in wonderful condition.
总之，我们认为我们都同情剧中的女主人公。	**In the final analysis**, I think our sympathy lies with the heroine of the play.
总之，那是个很繁华的地方。	It was a magnificent place **altogether**.
总之，这给他们大大增了光。	**All told**, it was a great credit to them.
总之，这样做是最好不过的。	It is best to do so **on every account**.
总之，这计划很好。	The plan was far better **on all accounts**.
总之，他不予以回答。	**At all events**, he gives no reply.
总之，是很成功的。	**All in all**, it was a great success.
总之，这周末非常好玩。	The weekend was, **in all**, a very enjoyable one.
总之，这个人没有教书的天才。	**The long and the short of the matter** is that the man is no teacher.
总之，那计划告吹了。	**The long and short of it** is that the plan was a failure.
总之，其病情显示极复杂。	**As a whole**, her ailment appeared to be extremely complicated.
总之我有点想买它。	I've half a mind to buy it **after all**.
总之,他并不缺钱。	**In any case**, he doesn't lack money.
总之，这是很大的成功。	**To conclude**, it was a great success.
总之，他终于娶了她。	**Anyhow**, he eventually married her.
总之，他已经死了。没有人能使他复活。	And **anyway** he was dead. Nobody could bring him back to life.

总之，我对一切都很厌倦。	**Overall**, I am tired of everything.
我打牌、看书、散步——总之，做所有的事情来使自己不去想那自知必须要做的决定。	I played cards, read, went for a walk — anything to take my thoughts off the decision I knew I must make.
目前的情况总之就是这样。	That's how things stack up today.
总之，请尽快做这件事。	If not now, please do so as soon as possible.

　　"总之"的英译，可谓花样翻新。在最后三个译例中，"总之"省译。翻译，无论英汉翻译，抑或汉英翻译，均忌对号入座。这种对号入座的做法，正是初学翻译者的陋习或积习之一。同词异译，正是改掉对号入座的翻译陋习的方法或技巧之一。而欲做到汉译英中的这种变化，就需要大量的阅读和积累，并善加利用。

七、古典诗词断句英译

　　有时，偶然读到一个英文句子，就会想起一首古诗或者古诗里的某个句子。例如：

The river nestling up to Auntie's village zigzagged from west to east,
it was a place of seductive charm all year round.

　　姥姥家那条河自西向东沿着庄子划了个曲里拐弯的弧，一年四季都在勾引人。

　　这就想起杜甫《江村》中的开头两行：

清江一曲抱村流，
长夏江村事事幽。

　　许渊冲英译如下：

The winding clear river around the village flows;
We pass the long summer by riverside with ease.

　　这样英译，已经很好。但是，如果我们借用上引英文句子，可尝试英译如下：

A limpid river nestling up to the village
zigzags from west to east: a place of seductive
charm all year round. The long and languid
summer sees the villagers at great ease.

　　显然，文字冗长了，但同时，似乎也更多了英文的味道。其实，如果具备足够的中国古典诗词英译的阅读经验，便会感觉到这样的译文，更像是外国人的译文。而这种外国人翻译中国古诗的味道，或曰英文的味道，正是中国译者所缺失的或不足的。

再如，读到这样一个英文句子：

Every instant seemed an age whilst we waited. The wind came now in fierce bursts, and the snow was driven with fury as it swept upon us in circling eddies.

每一秒钟都像是一个世纪。风猛烈地刮着，雪花愤怒地盘旋，扫荡着我们。

就想起唐代诗人岑参的名篇《白雪歌送武判官归京》中的前两句：

北风卷地白草折，

胡天八月即飞雪。

那么，借用英文句子，尝试英译如下：

White grass is uprooted into tumbleweed by northern wind which comes in fierce bursts;

September sees snow being driven with fury as it sweeps across the sky in circling eddies.

当然，"胡天"之"胡"未译，为了诗行大致的整齐。此处信息的缺失，可在其它地方补译。许渊冲英译如下：

Snapping the pallid grass, the northern wind whirls low;

In the eighth moon the Tartar sky is filled with snow.

显然，译文简洁多了。不过，也寡淡多了。

其实，不仅古诗英译，汉语新诗的英译，也可借助英文阅读而提高译文的效果。

例如，晨读英文，读到这样的句子：

The eyes are blank. （眼神空洞。）

想起英译严建文的诗作《三月的巴黎印象》，其中两行诗句：

又如那些宫殿里的画像

空洞的眼神

及其英译：

Again like the portraits in the temple

The empty expression in the eyes

在英译之初，就不太满意 empty 这个单词，只是一时没有着落。读到这句英文之后，终于算是"单词奇遇记"了。改译如下：

Again like the portraits in the temple

The blank expression in the eyes

汉语"空洞"，并非对应 blank，但却是非常到位的译文。若不是读到这个英文句子，也就翻译成 empty 了事，但是，读到并用了 blank，才对译文真正满意。

王家新在其专著《在一颗名叫哈姆雷特的星下》中，曾引用杜甫《对雪》的翻译：

战哭多新鬼， 愁吟独老翁。 乱云低薄暮， 急雪舞回风。 瓢弃樽无绿， 炉存火似红。 数州消息断， 愁坐正书空。	Tumult, weeping, many new ghosts. Heartbroken, aging, alone, I sing To myself. Ragged mist settles In the spreading dusk. Snow skurries In the coiling wind. The wineglass Is spilled.The bottle is empty. The fire has gone out in the stove. Everywhere men speak in whispers. I brood on the uselessness of letters. （雷克斯洛斯　译）	战乱，哭泣，许多新鬼。 心碎，衰老，孤独，我独自 吟唱。乱云沉淀 在这漫延的黄昏中。薛疾飞 在旋转的风中。杯中酒 已洒了。酒樽空了。 炉中火已熄灭。 各地人人压低声音说话。 我思考文学多么无用。 （钟玲　译）

"这里的中文译文为钟玲的译文。我想，雷克斯洛斯真是与杜甫的一颗诗心达到了很深的契合，所以他才敢于那样翻译结尾两句。这样翻译可以说创造出了另一首诗，但是，却又正好与杜诗的精神相通！或者说，如果杜甫活在今天，我想这也正是他想说而未能说出的话！"[26] 是的，读当代英文，译中国古诗，目的正是要达到与古诗的精神相通，用流畅鲜活的当代英文，再现中国古代诗人的诗思，甚至他们"想说而未能说出的话"。只有这样，古诗英译才能取得相对的成功，才能在西方英语国家打开阅读的市场。

八、以古诗英译为目的的英文阅读

李运兴在其近著《英译中国名家散文选：汉英对照》的《前言》中说："以汉译英为目的的英语阅读应有别于为其他目的而进行的阅读。应该带着汉译

---

26 王家新，在一颗名叫哈姆雷特的星下［M］，北京：中国人民大学出版社，2012：317-318。

英实践中的问题读，用心留意可用来应对汉语某些词语、说法、句式、句构、修辞的表达方法。这种以汉译英为取向的阅读，会给你带来许许多多可参照的'因袭'资源。"[27]是的，以汉译英为目的的英语阅读，最为重要。只有这样，才能有效地提高我们汉译英的水平和质量。比如，以前曾讨论过《红楼梦》其中一句话的翻译问题：

"好好的哭什么？"

这是一个长辈对晚辈所说的话，表示了关心和体贴。而正是这种关心的语气，简直是无法译出来的。多年后，我们阅读劳伦斯（D. H. Lawrence）的名著《恋爱中的女人》（Women in Love）时，读到这样一个句子：

Gerald has followed in wonder, amid the booing, not having caught her misdeed.

杰拉德在一片嘘声中莫名其妙地追出来，他不知道戈珍有什么做得不对。

这里，介词短语 in wonder，似乎正可表达一种微妙的语气。于是，尝试英译"好好的哭什么？"：

"Why are you crying?" he asked, in wonder, and very gently.

著名翻译家刘士聪评曰："'好好的哭什么？'，引号之外处理: he asked, in wonder, and very gently，不仅译出了语气，也描画出了问者的神色，效果非常好。"

然后，又读到《恋爱中的女人》的另外两个句子：

... asked Gerald, in wondering excitement.

杰拉德不解地问。

... she said at length, in a voice of question and detachment.

她似问非问地说。

同样，介词短语 in wondering excitement 和 in a voice of question and detachment，也可表述一种关切的语气。于是，再译"好好的哭什么？"：

"Why are you crying?" he asked, in wondering puzzlement.

或者：

"Why are you crying?" he asked, in a voice of wonder and

27 李运兴，前言［A］，李运兴，英译中国名家散文选：汉英对照［Z］，上海：上海外语教育出版社，2019。

solicitude.

或者：

"Why are you crying?" he asked, in a voice of concern and wonder.

著名翻译家刘士聪说："都有可取之处，看来有多种译法。好的表达方式多从阅读中来。"

后来，晨读英文，读到这样一个句子：

There was a wondering note in his voice.

便又想起《红楼梦》中"好好的哭什么？"似可另译如下：

"Why are you crying?" he asked. There was a wondering note in his
voice.

增译的句子 There was a wondering note in his voice，正是对原文暗含关切语气的解释和补充。

又读到这样一句英文：

I heartily wonder what they thought of us.

我很好奇，想知道他们是怎样看待我们的。

"好好的哭什么？"可另译如下：

I heartily wonder why you are crying.

再如，晨读英文，读到这样的句子：

How fresh and marvelous it all is, though spring is repeated every
year!

受到其中 repeated 一词的启发，想起以前讨论过的一副汉语对联的翻译：

年年岁岁花相似，

岁岁年年人不同。

觉得译出大意容易，但要译出味道很难。借鉴上句英文，试译如下：

From year to year flowers repeat themselves;

Annually we age and never remain ourselves.

这样，读来译文明显有所进步。

实践篇

（1）望庐山瀑布（李白）

先看这样一首英文诗及其汉译：

Potala Palace, Lhasa　　Patricia Prime (New Zealand)	拉萨的布达拉宫　帕特里夏·普赖姆（新西兰）
Potala Palace	布达拉宫
was a postcard	犹如一张明信片
Pinned against	别在湛蓝的天空
a blue sky	多冷啊
So cold	只听见
all you heard	河滩上牦牛和驴儿铃响叮当
was the sound of yak and donkey bells	飘过绿色河面
jangling on the river flats	回荡在莽莽荒野之上
over the green river	（刘文杰　译）[1]
out through bare fields.	

"一张明信片"，"别在湛蓝的天空"，当然是非常诗意的表达。英文 Pinned against，当然巧妙。这就让我们想起李白《望庐山瀑布》及其英译：

　　　望庐山瀑布　李白

　　日照香炉生紫烟，遥看瀑布挂前川。

　　飞流直下三千尺，疑是银河落九天。

1　刘文杰，英语诗歌汉译与赏析［Z］，广州：中山大学出版社，2014：23。

Watching the Waterfall at Lushan　Li Bai

In sunshine Censer Peak breathes purple vapour,

Far off hangs the cataract, a stream upended;

Down it cascades a sheer three thousand feet —

As if the Silver River were falling from Heaven!

（杨宪益、戴乃迭　译）[2]

The Waterfall in Mount Lu Viewed from Afar　Li Bai

The sunlit Censer Peak exhales incense-like cloud,

The cataract hangs like upended stream sounding loud.

Its torrent dashes down three thousand feet from high

As if the Silver River fell from azure sky.

（许渊冲　译）[3]

The Waterfall in Mount Lu Viewed from Afar　Li Bai

The sunlit Censer Peak exhales incenselike cloud,

Like an upended stream the cataract sounds loud.

Its torrent dashes down three thousand feet from high

As if the Silver River fell from the blue sky.

（许渊冲　译）[4]

Viewing the Waterfall at Mount Lu　Li Bai

Sunlight streaming on Incense Stone kindles a violet smoke;

Far off I watch the waterfall plunge to the long river,

Flying waters descending straight three thousand feet,

Till I think the Milky Way has tumbled from the ninth height of

Heaven.

（Burton Watson　译）[5]

2　Yang Xianyi & Gladys Yang. Poetry and Prose of the Tang and Song[Z]. Beijing: Chinese Literature Press, 1984: 33.

3　许渊冲，许渊冲英译李白诗选：汉英对照 ［Z］，北京：中国对外翻译出版有限公司，2014: 15。

4　许渊冲，唐诗三百首：汉英对照 ［Z］，北京：海豚出版社，2013: 46。

5　郭著章等，唐诗精品百首英译（修订版）［Z］，武汉：武汉大学出版社，2010: 62。

Viewing the Lushan Mountain Waterfall　Li Bai

Shines the sun on Xianglu Peak, generating a purple mist.

Viewed from afar, the falls hang down over the cliff,

Flying water makes a straight descent of three thousand feet,

Wonder if it's the Silver River plunging from the empyrean.

（任治稷、余正　译）[6]

"遥看瀑布挂前川"之"挂"，何其形象，何其生动传神！反观上引六种译文，多译为 hang，或者未译。就局部而言，翻译不能算是成功。卓振英说："针对汉诗诗学的这一特点，我们在汉诗英译的过程中就必须词斟句酌，相应地在译文语言的词句上反复锤炼、推敲，以求保持和再现原诗的意象、意境、音韵和节奏等诗歌美学价值，再创造出形神兼备的译品。这就是'炼词'。"[7]是的，写诗，讲究炼字炼词；翻译，同样需要炼字炼词。而翻译的炼字炼词，一般源语英文阅读中的"因袭资源"。终于，我们看到了如下英译：

Two Poems about Watching the Waterfall of Mount Lu (2)

Incense Burner is curling with

purple smoke in the sunshine.

A waterfall pours into the river:

Viewed from afar it is like a piece of

white cloth pinned against the cliff,

Hanging three thousand feet,

Which is suggestive of the Milky Way

tumbling down from heaven.

（张智中　译）[8]

显然，英译中 a piece of white cloth pinned against the cliff，是受到 *Potala Palace, Lhasa* 这首英译的启发下才译出的。

后来，我们又读到这样的英文句子：

He had **pinned** her in his arms in order to break the news.

6　任治稷、余正，从诗到诗：中国古诗词英译［Z］，北京：外语教学与研究出版社，2006：43。

7　卓振英、李贵苍，汉诗英译教程［M］，北京：北京大学出版社，2013：184。

8　张智中，李白绝句英译：英汉对照［Z］，北京：商务印书馆国际有限公司，2021：108。

他要用力抱着莫琳才让她听完了消息。

这里的动词 pin，"固定"、"牢靠"之意，也很形象。霍克斯英译《红楼梦》第十三回，也有动词 pin 的运用：

> 眼见不日又有一件非常的喜事，真是烈火烹油、鲜花着锦之盛。

> It will be a glory as excessive and as transitory as a posy of fresh flowers **pinned** to an embroidered dress or the flare-up of spilt cooking-oil on a blazing fire.

（2）相见欢 · 乌夜啼（李煜）

相见欢 · 乌夜啼　李煜	**Tune: Crows Crying at Night**　Li Yu
无言独上西楼， 月如钩。 寂寞梧桐深院锁清秋。 剪不断，理还乱， 是离愁。 别是一般滋味在心头。	Silent, I go up to the west tower alone and see the hooklike moon. The plane trees lonesome and drear, lock in the courtyard autumn clear. Cut, it won't break; Ruled, it will make A mess to wake An unspeakable taste in the heart. Such is the grief to part. （许渊冲　译）[9]

许渊冲先生的译文，从多数中国读者的角度，一般都觉得很好，所谓音美、形美、意美"三美"齐备。但是，其译文却一直主要在中国出版发行，没有在真正意义上走向西方。原因之一，我们以为，就是许渊冲的译诗语言，多是自己写出来的语言，较少英文精华之借用。

Donna Dailey 所著 *Charles Dickens* 中，有这样一个句子：

> To try **to purge his grief**, he took long walks through the city at night, visiting the darker areas around prisons, workhouses, and asylums.

这个英文句子中，动词 purge 及其宾语 grief 的搭配，何其鲜活有力！不是正可以用来表述李煜那无处倾诉无处排遣的离愁吗？

Susan Muaddi Darraj 所著 *Amy Tan* 中，有这样一个句子：

> The deaths of her father and brother **weighed heavily on Amy's**

9　许渊冲，唐五代词选：汉英对照［Z］，北京：海豚出版社，2013：99。

mind.

这里，weigh heavily on 及其宾语 mind 所表达的意思，在古典汉语诗词里何其常见。而我们在阅读古诗英译之时，却很难见到这样的措词，正是"别是一般滋味在心头"了。

再看是两个英文例子：

> … and after several **ineffectual** attempts to catch them in the tin bucket he forbore.

> 他用白铁桶去逮，试了好几次都无济于事。

> He watched the flying fish burst out again and again and the **ineffectual** movements of the bird.

> 眼前，飞鱼不时跳出水面，鸟儿次次扑空。

第一个句子里的 ineffectual，显然对应汉译"无济于事"；第二个句子里的 ineffectual，对应汉语"扑空"。李煜的"剪不断，理还乱"，不正是虽其"无言独上西楼"，而仍然"无济于事"或"扑空"的吗？

好了，如果我们因袭如上三个英文资源，李煜之《相见欢》，似可英译如下：

> **Joy at Meeting**　Li Yu
>
> Wordless, I mount the West Tower:
>
> a hook is the moon.
>
> Lonely parasol trees in the deep courtyard,
>
> where a clear autumn has been locked.
>
> Cutting, it is still connecting;
>
> combing, it is still entangling.
>
> This parting grief, where to purge?
>
> The attempts have been ineffectual:
>
> it weighs heavily on my mind,
>
> unnameable, unutterable,
>
> and untellable.
>
> （张智中　译）

译文中，"This parting grief, where to purge?" "it weighs heavily on my mind"，"The attempts have been ineffectual"，正是阅读英

文而化用的结果。

有时，英文中的一个小词，不为我们所注意，但却可能会有非常好的妙用。其实，上引 ineffectual 的词根，是 effect。我们不妨再来看关于 effect 一词的运用：

Diligent care has been taken to select such words as might least interrupt the **effect** of the beautiful English tongue in which he wrote.

我们也仔细斟酌，竭力做到不至于损害莎士比亚那样漂亮的英文。

显然，汉语译文中，effect 并未体现出来，因其含义微妙。如果我们倒过来，从汉译英的角度来看，一般的译者是想不起来添加这么一个 effect 的。而一旦有译者这样添加了，便非一般之译者。其实，这句英文来自 *Tales of Shakespeare*（《莎士比亚戏剧故事》），作者是英国著名散文家 Charles Lamb，文笔超好。再看英文句子：

It was brilliant moonlight, and the soft **effect** of the light over the sea and sky — merged together in one great, silent mystery — was beautiful beyond words.

天上有一轮明月，柔和的月光洒在天空中，流泻于海上。这种巨大而寂静的神秘力量将天地之间融合在了一起，此等美景真是难以用笔墨来形容。

这里的 effect，上引例子中的 effect，具同一美学效果。从不同的英文小说里，我们可以读到类似的 effect 的运用：

I see, by those light clouds in the west, there will be a brilliant sunset, and we shall be in time to witness its **effect** upon the sea, at the most moderate rate of progression.

从西方那些明亮的云彩来看，落日的景致一定会非常美丽的，我们走得再慢也能及时看到海上的落日。

有时，effect 的变形，包括 ineffectual 和 effectually 等，同样值得玩味。例如：

The sun was low and yellow, sinking down, and in the sky floated a thin, **ineffectual** moon.

金黄的夕阳正在西沉，天上漂浮起一圈淡淡的月影。

这里，ineffectual moon，"无效的月亮"，其实就指在白天几乎看不到的不起眼的月亮。汉译"淡淡的"，并不与之对应，也是无可奈何之译了。

> And he made the crew ply their oars so **effectually**, that the vessel
> flew through the water, quicker than a bird cleaves in the air.

这里法国作家伏尔泰（Voltair）的小说《老实人》（Candide, or, the Optimist）中的一个句子。作为译文的英文，却很漂亮，像英文原创一样地道。这里的 effectually（有效地），描写划桨的动作，非常得力，所以船的速度很快。

副词 effectually，在英文小说里见到另一应用：

> They found that he had **effectually** executed his duties.
> 他们发现这时他已经尽心尽力地把事情都安排妥当了。

这里，effectually 的汉译，自然是"尽心尽力"。但是，如果我们仔细品味，effectually 其实还是"有效果地"之意。执行任务有效，便引申为"尽心尽力"。

> They were quite unsteady when they came out, owing to the **effect**
> of the alcohol on their empty stomachs. It was a fine, mild day, and a
> gentle breeze fanned their faces.
> 因为空肚喝酒，所以出来时，他们都摇摇晃晃的。天气温暖宜
> 人，一阵和风拂面而来。

句中，the effect of the alcohol on their empty stomachs，描写空腹喝酒，酒精起了作用。英文小词 effect，非常难得。

体悟了以上英文句子中 effect 的妙用之后，我们来看李清照的《如梦令》：

> 昨夜雨疏风骤，浓睡不消残酒。
> 试问卷帘人，却道海棠依旧。
> 知否，知否？应是绿肥红瘦。

及其两种英译：

英译一：

Tune: Dreamlike Song

Last night the strong wind blew with a rain fine;

Sound sleep did not dispel the aftertaste of wine.

I ask the maid rolling up the screen.

"The same crab apple," says she, "can be seen."

"But don't you know,

Oh, don't you know

The red should languish and the green should grow?

（许渊冲　译）[10]

英译二：

A Dreamy Strain

The rain was light but the wind fierce yestereve;

Wine's effect on me my sound sleep didn't relieve.

I ask about th'begonias on which I'm keen.

"They're as nice as before," says the maid, rolling up th' screen.

"Do you know?

Do you know?"

Retort I, "What's red should be paler than what's green."

（卓振英　译）[11]

其中，"残酒"，英译一译为 the aftertaste of wine（酒的后味），"浓睡"之人，乃是酒醉之人，哪里还有什么酒的后味可言呢？显然偏颇。英译二 wine's effect（酒的影响或作用），正得其中。这与上引最后一个英文句子中 the effect of the alcohol on their empty stomachs，非常相近。

（3）滁州西涧（韦应物）

汉译英之时，若能用上一般译者意想不到的恰当之词，最见译者功夫，如韦应物的这首名诗及原来的英译：

| 滁州西涧　韦应物
独怜幽草涧边生，
上有黄鹂深树鸣。
春潮带雨晚来急，
野渡无人舟自横。 | **The West Creek at Chuzhou**　Wei Yingwu
Lovely grass grows by a secluded
creek, where orioles are twittering
in the foliage of trees. Spring tide,
with rainfall, runs fast at eventide;
at the deserted ferry,
a boat is swinging
by itself.
（张智中　译） |

---

10 许渊冲，宋词三百首：汉英对照［Z］，北京：海豚出版社，2013：132。

11 卓振英，英译宋词集萃：汉英对照［Z］，上海：上海外语教育出版社，2008：87。

在李煜《相见欢·乌夜啼》的英译中，我们讨论了 ineffectual 及其变形词汇的妙用，其实，有时一个句子，会有两个单词都使用得非常巧妙，令人回味。例如：

Two boats paddled near, their lanterns swinging **ineffectually**, the boats **nosing** round.

两条小船划近了，船上的灯照来照去一点都不管用。船在打着转。

关于 ineffectual（"无效果的；徒劳无益的；不起作用的"），另例如下：

An **ineffectual** remedy.

无效的药物。

Ineffectual efforts.

徒劳的努力。

Most of those remaining are **ineffectual**.

剩下的人大多是起不了什么作用的。

动词 nose，意为"用鼻子推；（船等）小心翼翼地（慢慢地）前进。"例如：

The boat **nosed** its way through the fog.

船在雾中缓缓前进。

The little boat **nosed** carefully between the rocks.

小船在礁石间小心翼翼地穿行。

The car **nosed** to the curb outside the apartment building.

汽车向公寓大楼外的路边靠拢。

那么，《滁州西涧》可改译如下，并回译成汉语：

The West Creek at Chuzhou　Wei Yingwu	滁州西涧　韦应物
Lushly green grass grows by a secluded creek, where orioles are twittering in the foliage of trees. Spring tide, with rainfall, runs fast at eventide; at the deserted ferry, a little boat is nosing round, swinging by itself ineffectually. （张智中　译）	青翠的嫩草生长在幽幽 的溪边，黄鹂啼鸣 浓密的树叶间。春潮， 带雨，晚来，流急； 荒弃的渡口，一个 小船打转，独自 轻摇轻摆， 摇摆。 （张智中　译）

添加或移植了副词 ineffectually，诗意效果又得以增加。如果不是细读了多个含有 effect 或其变形 effectual 的英语句子，我们便很难体会到改译中 ineffectually 的运用之妙。

伏尔泰（Voltair）小说《老实人》中的英文句子：And he made the crew ply their oars so **effectually**, that the vessel flew through the water, quicker than a bird cleaves in the air.

副词 effectually，正写划船之有效和得力。而这里的"野渡无人舟自横"，似可反其意而用之：ineffectually。于是，《滁州西涧》另译如下：

The West Creek at Chuzhou　Wei Yingwu

Lovely lush green grass grows by a secluded creek,

above which orioles are twittering in the foliage

of trees. Spring tide, under the cover of a

rainfall, runs fast at eventide; at the

deserted ferry, a boat, by itself,

is swinging about wildly and

ineffectually amid an

eddy of torrential

water.

（张智中　译）

如上英译中，under the cover of a rainfall（在雨幕的掩护之下），写涧边之雨景，颇具诗意。随后的 a boat, by itself, is swinging about wildly and ineffectually amid an eddy of torrential water，改写自这样一个英文句子：

A swan in deadly alarm **swims wildly about amid an eddy of** bloody feathers.

一只惊恐万状的天鹅在血色的旋涡中打转，拼命地乱游。

下面句子中的动词 eddy，同样形象生动。

But these thoughts are not my thoughts; they **eddy** through my mind like scraps of old paper, or withered leaves in the wind.

但是这些思想并非我的思想，它们像风中的旧纸片或枯叶般在我的脑海中旋转着飞过。

好了，让我们忘记之前的译文，再来阅读英文：

As the night set in it grew **blustering** and gusty.

夜幕降临，狂风咆哮。

"春潮带雨晚来急"的英译，可以考虑使用动词 bluster（咆哮；风狂吹；夸口）或其形容词形式 blustery（大风的；猛烈的；狂暴的）。

又读到一个短语：

A gusty storm with **strong sudden rushes of** wind.

觉得 strong sudden rushes of 的表述，生动有力，可译"春潮""晚来急"之状貌。

下面的英文句子，亮点都是 animation 或 animated：

All **animation** had gone from her face.

她脸上生气全无。

It was a scene of great **animation** and confusion.

屋里人们舞成一团。

It gave me pleasure to see him **animated** with the prospect of making a fortune and then returning to Scotland.

我很高兴看到他因为充满了希望而富有朝气和活力。

The voice of Mrs Salmon shrilled against the noise of the birds, which rose ever more wild and triumphant, and the woman's voice went up and up against them, and the birds replied with wild **animation**.

赛尔蒙太太提高嗓门，鸟儿们似乎在跟她对着干，叫得更起劲儿了。

I said I would not, and he related the following strange adventure, speaking sometimes with **animation**, sometimes with melancholy, but always with feeling and earnestness.

我说我不会的，于是他讲述了下面那段离奇的经历，时而说得生动活泼，时而说得忧郁沮丧，但始终情绪饱满、郑重其事。

显然，animation 或 animated，在古诗英译中，似乎大有可为。综合考虑之后，韦应物《滁州西涧》另译如下：

The West Creek at Chuzhou　Wei Yingwu

Lovely lush green grass grows

　　by a secluded creek, above

which orioles are twittering

in the thick foliage of trees.

Spring tide, under the cover

of a sky which is blustery,

blusterous, and blustering,

is running in strong sudden

rushes of water when the ferry,

deserted to be soulless, is

animated by a small boat —

nosing round by itself

against the current,

wildly and ineffectually,

amid a murky eddy

of torrential water.

（张智中　译）

译诗中，多处借用或化用，其中，由动词 bluster（咆哮；风狂吹；夸口）衍生出三个不同的形容词：blustery（大风的；猛烈的；狂暴的），blusterous（狂吹的；叫嚷的；咆哮的），blustering（汹涌的；狂风大作的；狂暴的），并而用之，极写"春潮带雨晚来急"之狂野状貌，同时带来音韵效果。比读《滁州西涧》的另外三种英译：

On the West Stream at Chuzhou

Alone, I like the riverside where green grass grows

And golden orioles sing amid the leafy trees.

When showers fall at dusk, the river overflows;

A lonely boat athwart the ferry floats at ease.

（许渊冲　译）[12]

AT WEST CREEK IN CH'U-CHOU

Alone, I savor wildflowers tucked in along the creek,

and there's a yellow oriole singing in treetop depths.

---

12 许渊冲，唐诗三百首：汉英对照［Z］，北京：海豚出版社，2013：111。

Spring floods come rain-swollen and wild at twilight.

No one here at the ferry, a boat drifts across of itself.

（David Hinton　译）[13]

Superseded

Alas for the lonely plant that grows beside the river bed,

While the mango-bird screams loud and long from the tall tree overhead!

Full with the freshets of the spring, the torrent rushes on;

The ferry-boat swings idly, for the ferryman is gone.

（H. A. Giles　译）[14]

"独怜幽草涧边生"，许渊冲的英译好理解，David Hinton 的英译却不太好理解：Alone, I savor wildflowers tucked in along the creek, 其中：

tuck: 打摺；卷起；收拢；藏起；<俚>大吃。

tuck in: 塞入；大吃一顿。

回译汉语，大概如此：

"孤独一人，我沿路欣赏着小溪折叠着的野花"。

如果说这是中国某个诗人的创作，也该是一句靓丽的诗行了吧。靓就靓在，"折叠着的野花"（wildflowers tucked in）。以花译草，当然不忠。但，若画家作画，以"独怜幽草涧边生"为题，说能禁止画家不绘出几朵小花来呢？况且，"春潮带雨"之时，"上有黄鹂深树鸣"，若配之以花，则更添画面之美。若视译诗如作画，则辛顿（David Hinton）此译不误。

接下来，in treetop depths, rain-swollen, wild at twilight, 用词何等鲜活而诗意丰盈！只是，将"舟自横"译为 a boat drifts across of itself（一只小船独自漂流过河）——副词 across 的使用，将相对静止的小船，变成"漂洋过海"达到彼岸的小船了。总之，David Hinton 的译文，多处亮点，值得学习。

Giles 的译文开头即用 Alas，应该是对"独怜幽草涧边生"中"怜"（"可爱"之意）的误解误读和误译。整首诗的翻译，最多是寡味的散文。尤其最后一行"野渡无人舟自横"的英译：The ferry-boat swings idly, for the ferryman is

13 David Hinton. Classical Chinese Poetry: An Anthology[Z]. New York: Farrar, Straus and Giroux, 2008: 288.

14 杨洋，古意新声：初级本 [C]，武汉：湖北教育出版社，2002: 88-89。

gone.（渡船空转着，因为摆渡者走了。）说明译者没有理解这首诗的深意。

再回首，似乎还是运用劳伦斯的 ineffectually，效果更好——小船晃悠悠，只在水边洲。

（4）小雨（杨万里）

无独有偶，在英译宋人杨万里的一首绝句时，又忽然想起 ineffectually：

小雨	**A Slight Rain**
雨来细细复疏疏， 纵不能多不肯无。 似妒诗人山入眼， 千峰故隔一帘珠。	A slight rain is sprinkling, spraying, drizzling, drozzling, like fine incessant needles of water which are playing in the air, before drifting down, instead of tapering off. Jealous of the poet's eyeful of green mountains which are dim and distant? A curtain of beads of rain is made, to screen off peaks upon peaks, ineffectually. （张智中　译）

诗写小雨，真是清新可爱。前两行描写小雨的样子，惟妙惟肖；后两行采取拟人，好像诗人看山而不厌，雨幕珠帘产生了嫉妒之意，便欲挡住诗人的视线。

英译首先采用 sprinkling, spraying, drizzling, drozzling 等四个带 -ing 后缀的词语，来描写小雨飘洒之状貌。随后的比喻 like fine incessant needles of water，来自英文阅读：

Through one of the broken panes I heard the rain impinging upon the earth, **the fine incessant needles of water** playing in the sodden beds.

透过破碎的玻璃窗，我听到雨密密麻麻地泻在土地上，像针似的细雨在湿透了的泥土上不断跳跃。

而 tapering off 则来自《新英汉词典》上的例句：taper off，逐渐减少（变弱），逐渐停止。例句：

The population growth is **tapering off**.

人口增长在逐渐减慢。

后面的 A curtain of beads of rain is made，改写自这两个英文句子：

Time was dripping into **beads of rain** outside.

钟表嘀嗒不断，化成窗外涟涟的雨滴。

The shower was so thick that it made **a curtain of rain**.

阵雨密密麻麻，织成了雨帘。

至于动词短语 to screen off（用屏风隔开），同样来自英文的启发：

A bookcase **screens off** part of the room.

有个书柜把房间隔开了一部分。

Screen off her bed and make sure she's not disturbed.

将她的床用屏风隔开，以确保她不受任何干扰。

当然，最重要的，该是最后一个副词 ineffectually（徒劳地；无效地）的添加——雨幕珠帘遮不住，秀山丽峰入眼来。

（5）生查子 · 元夕（欧阳修）

同由 effect 派生而出的形容词 effectual，在古诗词的英译中，可起到微妙的美学作用。例如，欧阳修这首著名的词及其英译：

生查子 · 元夕　欧阳修

去年元夜时，花市灯如昼。

月上柳梢头，人约黄昏后。

今年元夜时，月与灯依旧。

不见去年人，泪湿春衫袖。

Lantern Festival Again　Ouyang Xiu

Last year, last lantern festival,

the flowery fair is brilliantly lit like a broad

day: my sweetie and I meet after the afternoon,

when the moon is effectual through the willows ...

This year, this evening, as it darkens a variety of gay-colored

lamps are lit as brilliantly as the moon, casting rays of light,

which fails to fall full upon her fair face —

I am beside myself with sentimentality,

and my spring sleeves are soaked

with tears dripping

and dropping

...

（张智中　译）

译诗第四行 when the moon is effectual through the willows 中，effectual 的含义和妙用，恐怕不为一般读者所能理解和感悟。我们不妨再回顾一下前面引用过的英文句子：

The sun was low and yellow, sinking down, and in the sky floated a thin, **ineffectual** moon.

金黄的夕阳正在西沉，天上漂浮起一圈淡淡的月影。

其实，这个句子来自英国著名作家劳伦斯的名著《恋爱中的女人》（*Women in Love*）。夕阳西沉之时，空中的月亮，真的可谓惨兮淡兮，几乎隐形不见。因此，形容词 ineffectual（无效的；白费的）可谓描写传神，非汉语"淡淡"所能对应。

这里，"月上柳梢头"，或"人约黄昏后"之时，与劳伦斯"金黄的夕阳正在西沉"之时，恰好时间上几乎吻合，或者更确切一点的话，我们可以说，欧阳修的时间更靠后一点，似乎将近"半个月亮爬上来"之时。因此，英译为 when the moon is effectual through the willows（当月亮开始在柳梢枝头显现）。注意，如果逆向思维，表示月亮之"显现"，一般译者可能会用 appear 之类的动词，则效果差矣。

另外，译诗第二个诗节中 as it darkens a variety of gay-colored lamps are lit as brilliantly as the moon，借鉴自如下英文句子：

Music and singing were going on, and as **the evening darkened hundreds of gay-colored lamps were lit**.

音乐和歌声持续着，当夕阳余晖逐渐变得昏暗的时候，数以百计各式各样的灯就被点亮了起来。

接下来第三行 which fails to fall full upon her fair face，头韵效果明显，借鉴自这个英文句子：

…where a wandering shaft of **light fell full upon** the golden allamanda, …

不经意的一束阳光洒落在金黄色的黄蔓……

可以说，读英文，悟其精髓，并巧妙运用，方显译者本领。有了英文的借用，译诗便有了英诗的味道。

（6）题临安邸（林升）

题林安邸

山外青山楼外楼，西湖歌舞几时休？

暖风熏得游人醉，直把杭州作汴州。

下面这些从英文阅读得来的句子，都可以联想到此诗：

The wind **brought us a noise of singing**.

随着微风飘来一阵像歌声。

Next door there appeared to be a children's party, for **the merry buzz of young voices and the clatter of a piano resounded through the night**.

隔壁好像是儿童聚会，欢快稚嫩的喊喊喳喳声和丁丁冬冬的钢琴声在夜幕中回荡。

Then the trees closed up again, and they went on and up, **with trumpetings and crashings, and the sound of breaking branches on every side of them**.

接着树丛又合上了，他们继续往上走，周围不停地传来吼叫声、撞击声和树枝断裂的声音。

The air was **full of their scent**, sweet and heady.

空气里洋溢着花香，其甜美熏人欲醉。

Indeed, after **a moderate share of the pleasures of London**, a man has a much better chance to make a rational unprejudiced marriage.

所以当一个人在伦敦过了一段纸醉金迷的生活后，最好的选择就是老老实实结婚。

The English visitors could hear **the occasional twanging of a zither, the strumming of a piano, snatches of laughter and shouting and singing, a faint vibration of voices**.

英国人听得到偶然传来的奇特琴声、漫不经心敲出来的钢琴声和说笑、喊叫及歌声，不过听不大清。

Towards afternoon **we got fairly drunken with the sunshine and the exhilaration of the pace**. We could no longer contain ourselves and our content.

快到下午的时候我们完全陶醉在阳光和愉快的航行之中。我们再也不能抑制自己的心满意足。

在上面句子中，a noise of singing，voices …resounded through the night，with trumpetings and crashings, and the sound of breaking branches on every side of them，the air was full of their scent, sweet and heady，a moderate share of the pleasures of，the occasional twanging of a zither, the strumming of a piano, snatches of laughter and shouting and singing, a faint vibration of voices，we got fairly drunken with the sunshine and the exhilaration of the pace 等对于各种声音的描写，以及陶醉于欢笑声的描写，恰好可以改造，来用于英译《题临安邸》：

Written in an Inn of the New Capital　Lin Sheng

Hills beyond blue hills,

mansions upon mansions;

in the warm wind there is a faint vibration

of occasional noises of trumpeting, twanging,

strumming, singing, dancing, and snatches of laughter,

resounding through the West Lake,

when to rest?

In such a charming air,

the travelers are fairly heady

and drunken with all this exhilaration;

an immoderate share of the pleasures of Hangzhou

deprives them of the fond memory of their old capital.

（张智中　译）

我们不妨比较许渊冲的英译：

Written at the New Capital

Hills rise beyond blue hills; towers beyond high towers.

When will West Lake end its singing and dancing hours?

The revelers are drunk with vernal breeze and leisure;

They'd seek in the new capital for their lost pleasure.

（许渊冲　译）[15]

从文体简洁风格的角度来看，许渊冲的译诗是可取的。但是，如果作为独立的英文诗来看的话，前面我们借鉴英文的翻译，或许更能赢得英语读者的青睐。

（7）约客（赵师秀）

黄梅时节家家雨，青草池塘处处蛙。

有约不来过夜半，闲敲棋子落灯花。

如果我们心里想着这首诗，来读英文：

And after another few dances, **the night being well run on**, the queen gave ending to this first day's recreation.

大家又跳了一会舞，夜色愈加浓了，女王便下令结束第一天的娱乐。

Then his daughter may negligently throw him a few moments of charming cajolery. He may gossip **in simple idleness** with his wife.

然后女儿可能心不在焉地对他说些甜言蜜语，他也可能和妻子懒洋洋地说点闲话。

It is a treatment easier to practice during daylight, in company, when distractions are plentiful, than **in the solitude of the night**.

这个方法在白天比较容易执行，在公司里能让人分心的事情很多，但在夜里独自一人时就不那么容易了。

She **toyed with** an eraser.

她拿着一块橡皮擦在手上耍弄。

He **rapped his car keys on** the hard surface, **beating out wasted time**.

他百无聊赖地在台面上轻轻敲打着手中的车钥匙。

---

15 许渊冲，宋元明清诗选：汉英对照［Z］，北京：海豚出版社，2013：80。

She passed by the valet, **the smouldering candle flickered up**, and she saw clearly Prince Andrey, lying with his arms stretched out on the quilt, looking just as she had always seen him.

她走过随从身旁，蜡烛芯结的灯花掉下来，于是，她清楚地看见了手伸出被子的躺着的安德烈公爵，像她从前一向见到的那个样子。

这些英文句子中，the night being well run on，正是约客不来"过夜半"之时；in simple idleness，in the solitude of the night，正是"过夜半"而仍在等客之状貌；toyed with an eraser（chessman），beating out wasted time，正可写"闲敲棋子"之状貌；the smouldering candle flickered up，可绘"落灯花"之状态。借用如此英文表达，可得如下译文：

Waiting for My Playmate   Zhao Shixiu
The rainy season sees it raining from roof to roof;
grassy ponds, here and there, are alive with
croaking frogs. The night being well run
on, I am still waiting, in simple idleness,
for my playmate who fails to come;
I toy with the chessman by rapping
it on the table, to beat out wasted
time, the smouldering candle
flickering up through
the solitude of
the night.

（张智中　译）

又，读到这样的英文句子：

Audrey thumped the table in delight, just **hard enough to make** the cups, the pens and the tissue paper littering the solid surface **vibrate slightly**.

这样的描写，觉得正好写出"闲敲棋子落灯花"中的动作"敲"字。

又读到这样的英文句子或短语：

A **steady rain** fell all afternoon;

in the **streaming rain**;

Summer rain often forms a rainbow;

fall into **idleness**;

spend time **in idleness**;

A man, like a sword, rusts **in idleness**.

借鉴之后,《约客》另译如下,再比较许渊冲的英译:

Waiting in Idleness　Zhao Shixiu	**A Promise Unkept**　Zhao Shixiu
In a steadily streaming summer rain all roofs are caught, when grassy ponds, big and small, far and near, are noisy with croaking frogs. Midnight finds me waiting for my play- mate, and beating the table, in idleness, with a chessman, hard enough to make it vibrate slightly, the lamp flickering in the solitude of the night. （张智中　译）	In rainy season house on house is steeped in rain; On poolside meadow here and there frogs croak in vain. My friend's not kept his word to come, now it's midnight. What can I do but play chess alone by lamplight? （许渊冲　译）[16]

　　许渊冲的英译,正是文字"忠实"之译,包括尾韵等,都尽力忠实。其实,最后一行的 What can I do,似乎急不可耐,非诗人之本意。赵师秀《约客》之美,在其难以言喻的轻灵婉约:客虽不来,却不怨不恨,耐人寻味。当然,我们借助英文的冗长译文,可能有读者会认为发挥过度。这也要看是什么样的"度"了。如果译诗不悖诗意,只是译者深刻顿悟之后的诗意联想与发挥,与原诗保持了情趣的一致,译者就没有发挥过度,是而调整适度,或许恰到好处。

　　诗歌不能翻译,只能再创,此即明证。再创不同于原创之处,在于译诗是译者在原诗激发出的灵感之下的产物,而这种灵感包括诗意灵感和语言灵感。

---

16 许渊冲，宋元明清诗选：汉英对照 [Z]，北京：海豚出版社，2013：83。

（8）竹枝词二首（一）（刘禹锡）

竹枝词二首（一）　　刘禹锡	Two Bamboo Branch Songs (No.1)　　Liu Yuxi
杨柳青青江水平， 闻郎江上踏歌声。 东边日出西边雨， 道是无晴却有晴。	Green are poplars and willows, river water overflowing; a youngster is heard singing on the river. In the east, it shines; in the west, it rains; oh my sunshine; if not here, it is there. 　　　　（张智中　译）

英译中，oh my sunshine，来自一首著名的美国民歌：You Are My Sunshine（《你是我的太阳》），这里活用，正可资跨文化之联想。"东边"、"西边"，变通为 in the east 和 in the west，译出了"东边"和"西边"的动态感。接下来，if not here, it is there，这里的 here 与 there 不仅形成诗行内韵，还因其为习语 here and there 的活用而变得灵动起来，正像 in the east 和 in the west 一样。Here 与 there 的灵活使用，使得译诗有了俏皮的味道，在某种程度上传译了原诗"无晴"和"有晴"的双关之意。译诗回译：

> 青青的杨柳，
>
> 河水满溢着；
>
> 只听一个小伙子唱歌
>
> 在岸边。东边，
>
> 阳光灿烂；西边，
>
> 细雨蒙蒙；噢，我的阳光；
>
> 不在这儿，就在那儿。

算是一首现代化的译诗了。后来，又读到一句英文：

Sun and shower alternated like day and night, making the hours longer by their variety.

> 阳光和阵雨交替出现，就像昼夜交替一样，它们的变化使得时间变得更长。

显然，这个句子与"东边日出西边雨"有着天生的"血缘关系"。《竹枝词二首（一）》改译如下：

Two Bamboo Branch Songs (No. 1)　Liu Yuxi

Green are poplars and willows, river water

overflowing; a youngster is heard singing

on the river, where sun and shower

alternate like day and night.

In the east, it shines; in

the west, it rains; oh

my sunshine: if

not here, it is

there.

（张智中　译）

改译中，添加了 the sun and shower alternate like day and night（阳光和阵雨交替出现，就像昼夜交替一样），这正是翻译教材里常见的"合理添译"。又读到菲茨杰拉德（Fitzgerald）名著《了不起的盖茨比》（*The Great Gatsby*）中的一个句子：

The rain was still falling, but **the darkness had parted in the west**, and there was a pink and golden billow of foamy clouds above the sea.

雨还没有停，但西方的乌云已经散开，粉红色和金色的云霞在海湾的上空翻腾着。

借鉴后，另译刘禹锡《竹枝词二首（一）》如下，并比较许渊冲的英译：

Two Bamboo Branch Songs (No.1)　Liu Yuxi	**Bamboo Branch Songs (I)**　Liu Yuxi
Drooping willows, freshly green, are kissing river water which is overflowing. A youngster is heard singing on the river, where sun and shower alternate like day and night. In the west, the rain is still falling; in the east, the darkness has parted: oh, my sunshine,	Between the green willows the river flows along; My dear one in a boat is heard to sing a song. The west is veiled in rain, the east enjoys sunshine; My dear one is as deep in love as day is fine. （许渊冲　译）[17]

17 许渊冲，唐诗三百首：汉英对照［Z］，北京：海豚出版社，2013：125。

if not here, it is there — my sunshine never parts from me. （张智中　译）	

　　显然，两种风格的译诗了。笔者借用英文资源，笔法灵活；许译则中规中矩，竭力忠实传译。这种忠实，往往是诗歌形式上，包括诗行长短、尾韵等方面的忠实，以及诗歌文字字面上的忠实。但是，就诗歌翻译而言，这样的忠实是远远不够的。中国诗歌欲走向西方世界，必须重视诗意的忠实：汉语诗歌是一首经典的诗歌，英译也该是一首英诗的精品，至少应该是令西方读者感动的译作。如果译诗不能达到这样的效果，无论多么看起来多么忠实的翻译，都是不忠实的，至少是精神上不忠实的译作。诗歌之所以是诗歌，首先在于其充盈的诗意。译诗如果仅仅停留在形式上的忠实，而不能达到充沛的诗意忠实的话，译诗便很难取得真正的成功。

（9）登鹳雀楼（王之涣）

登鹳雀楼　王之涣	**On Stork and Magpie Tower**　Wang Zhihuan
白日依山尽， 黄河入海流。 欲穷千里目， 更上一层楼。	Way down behind the hills the sun is going; Into the sea the Yellow River's flowing. Wanting to see as far as my eyes could, Climb up still one more flight of stairs I should. （王大濂　译）[18]

　　译文押韵格式：aabb，但却为此付出了代价：除了第三行，其他三个诗行都采取倒装，显得造作而不太自然。

On the Stork Tower　Wang Zhihuan	**Going up the Stork Tower**　Wang Zhihuan
The sun along the mountain bows; The Yellow River seawards flows. You will enjoy a grander sight If you climb to a greater height. （许渊冲　译）[19]	The setting sun dips behind the mountains. The Yellow River rushes out to sea. For a better view of things out there, We need to climb one more flight of stair. （龚景浩　译）[20]

---

18 王大濂，英译唐诗绝句百首［Z］，天津：百花文艺出版社，1997：9。
19 许渊冲，唐诗三百首：汉英对照［Z］，北京：海豚出版社，2013：29。
20 龚景浩，英译唐诗名作选［Z］，北京：商务印书馆，2006：9。

许译显有进步。但是，除了押韵工整之外，从语言上来看，译文似乎并无多少亮点。

至于龚景浩译文，李赋宁在为译者写的《序》中说："'白日依山尽'，龚译为'The setting sun dips behind the mountains'，'dips'一词很有力。'欲穷千里目'译为'For a better view of things out there'，也用意译法。……我想好的译文一方面要译出原文的神韵，同时也要具有英诗的味道，读起来像英诗。"21

"具有英诗的味道，读起来像英诗"，就是译者要借用英文的表达方式，以使译文地道。如果我们查阅英汉词典，可读到这样的例句：

The sun **dipped** below the horizon.
太阳沉到地平线以下。

可见，"dips"一词之所以"很有力"，即在于其地道，是纯正的英文。在《登鹳雀楼》的众多英译中，一般译者想不起来用 dip 这个词的，龚译却用了，所以出彩。

读英汉词典，偶然碰到这样的例子：

The river **empties itself into** the Yellow Sea.
这条河流入黄海。

读英文小说，又见到这样的句子：

It was strange to see the snow falling in such heavy flakes close to us, and beyond, the sun shining more and more brightly as **it sank down towards the far mountain tops**.

很奇怪，我们眼前的雪下得很大，但是在它们的外面太阳越来越明亮。

… so I scrambled on until I had got so far that the topmost branch was bending beneath my weight … I found myself looking down at a most wonderful **panorama** of this strange country in which we found ourselves.

因此，我继续向上爬，爬到了最高处的树枝上，树枝在我的重压下都弯了下来。……我俯瞰着我们目前所在的这个神秘国度绝妙无比的全景，一切尽收眼底。

---

21 李赋宁，序［A］，龚景浩，英译唐诗名作选［Z］，北京：商务印书馆，2006。

于是有如下英译：

Ascending the Stork Tower　　Wang Zhihuan

The white sun is shining

and decaying as it sinks

down towards the far

mountain tops, when

the Yellow River empties

itself into the sea. To enjoy

a panoramic view, you can

climb to a greater height.

（张智中　译）

其实，英文的反身代词，构成英文语言的优势之一。有了这样的借用，译诗语言也就多了一点回味的余地。又读英文，得如下句子：

Now **daylight began to appear**.

天边出现了曙光。

The **light was dimming**.

天色昏暗了。

Early on the Sunday morning, the sun showed itself bright and lovely.

Its **golden beams** began to appear on the tops of the nearby mountains.

星期天一大早，阳光明媚，金色的光束洒向附近的山顶。

《登鹳雀楼》又可英译如下：

Ascending the Stork Tower　　Wang Zhihuan

The light is now dimming

　　as the golden beams of the sun

begin to disappear from the

　　tops of the distant mountains,

when the Yellow River empties

　　itself into the sea. To enjoy

a panoramic view, you can

　　climb to a greater height.

（张智中　译）

这样一来，"白日依山尽，黄河入海流"的英文，便更加形象，具画面之感。另外，译诗中最后一个单词 height，这里并非抽象的高度之意，而是具体的"高处；高地"之意。例如读英文小说得来的句子：

From the **height** where we were it was possible to see a great distance; and far off, beyond the white waste of snow, I could see the river lying like a black ribbon in kinks and curls as it wound its way.

在我们所站的**高地**上可以看到很远的距离——远远的在雪之外，我能看见一条蜿蜒的河，如弯曲的黑色缎带。

又读英文：

Delay **spells** losses.

拖延招致损失。

这里的动词 spell，意为"招致；带来；意味着"等。

He **feasted his eye on** the beautiful scene.

他尽情欣赏这美丽的景色。

注意，这里的 eye，用单数即可。例如：

Beauty is in the **eye** of the beholder.

情人眼里出西施。

Don't **slacken your efforts** till the work is done.

工作完成前别松劲。

借鉴如上英文，《登鹳雀楼》英译如下：

Ascending the Stork Tower　　Wang Zhihuan

The sun

ends behind

the mountain, which

does not spell the end of

running water: the Yellow River

is emptying itself into the sea. To feast

your eye on the boundless view, climb to a

greater height　—　never, never slacken your efforts.

（张智中　译）

译文中，除了借鉴之外，第一个 end 做动词，第二个 end 做名词，恰好表达诗中"白日"之"尽"与"黄河"之"流不尽"。再看下面两个英文句子：

The path has been cut half-way round the fall **to afford a complete view**, but it ends abruptly, and the traveller has to return as he came.

半山腰上，一条小径环绕瀑布辟出，使人能饱览瀑布全景，可是小径断然终止，游客只好原路返回。

句中，to afford a complete view 正是"欲穷千里目"的另类表达，虽然笼统，却也地道。

And then came to a little rising ground, which **gave me a full view of** them **at the distance of** about eighty yards.

那旁边有块小小的高地，距离他们大约有八十码远。站在上面，我能把他们的一举一动尽收眼底。

这里，gave me a full view of 与 afford a complete view 是同义短语，随后的 at the distance of，可表示距离之遥。若考虑运用这种表达，并采取诗体西化的译法的话，《登鹳雀楼》又有如下译文：

Ascending the Stork Tower　　Wang Zhihuan

The light is dimming as the

golden beams begin to disappear

from the tops of the distant

mountains, which are to swallow

up the white sun on the decaying.

The Yellow River charges

eastward, emptying itself into

the sea. To enjoy a panoramic

view　—　climb, climb to a great,

greater height, which affords a

complete view of the landscape at

the distance of thousands of miles.

（张智中　译）

（10）戏为六绝句（二）（杜甫）

晨读英文，读到这样的句子：

...our names should not perish with our bodies, but should **go**

down to posterity associated with the result of our labors.

我们的名字也不会同躯壳一般死亡，我们的后代会铭记我们的功绩。

就想起杜甫绝句及其原来的英译：

戏为六绝句（二） 杜甫 王杨卢骆当时体， 轻薄为文哂未休。 尔曹身与名俱灭， 不废江河万古流。	**Six Quartrains Composed in Jest (2)** Du Fu Wang, Yang, Lu and Luo have made contributions in the early Stage of Tang poetry, but some frivolous people are ridiculing Them. Soon your body and fame will perish, while their names And literary pieces, like endless rivers, will be running forever. （张智中 译）

吸取英语语言之精华，采取自由诗体，改译如下：

Six Quartrains Composed in Jest (2) Du Fu

Wang, Yang, Lu and Luo have made contributions

in the early stage of Tang poetry, but some

frivolous people are ridiculing them.

Soon your name will perish with

your body, while their names

and literary pieces will go

down to posterity, like

endless rivers which

are running

forever.

（张智中 译）

（11）池上二首（一）（白居易）

池上二首（一） 白居易 山僧对棋坐， 局上竹阴清。 映竹无人见， 时闻下子声。	**Over the Pond (No. 1 of two poems)** Bai Juyi Two mountain monks are sitting playing chess, chessboard checkered with sunlight and bamboo shade. Partitioned by bamboos, the players are unseeable; the sound of chessmen is heard now and then. （张智中 译）

读到英文句子：

As Cletus walked **into the cool shade of the house** he heard voices.

克莱图斯走进房子的阴凉处，他就听见各种声音。

The curtains **screen out** the sunlight.

窗帘遮住了阳光。

The camera lens must be **screened** from direct sunlight.

照相机的镜头不可受到阳光的直射。

这里的动词 screen，乃"掩蔽；遮蔽"之意。

In a very short while she heard him coming back to the house.

既然可以说 a very short while，也可以用其反义：once in a great while。

因此，整首诗改译如下：

Over the Pond (No. 1 of two poems)　　Bai Juyi

Sitting in the cool shade

　　of a bamboo grove, two

mountain monks are playing

　　chess. The chessboard is

checkered with sunlight

　　and bamboo shadow.

Screened by bamboos,

　　the players are unseeable;

only the sound of chessmen

　　is heard once in a great while.

（张智中　译）

后来，又读到《飘》（*Gone with the Wind*）中的一个句子：

The red road lay **checkered in shade and sun-glare** beneath the over-arching trees and the many hooves kicked up little red clouds of dust.

阳光在枝柯如拱的大树下闪烁，那条红土大道在树荫中光影斑驳，纷纷而过的马蹄扬起一阵阵云雾般的红色尘土。

此诗英译：The chessboard is checkered with sunlight and bamboo shadow，与《飘》中的 The red road lay checkered in shade and sun-glare 高度相似。介词 with 语法上来讲也不错，但似乎强调动作，介词 in 却表示状态。阳光与阴影，

构成一幅画面，一种静止的状态，当然 in 更好。读到这个英文句子，就知道白居易《池上二首（一）》中的介词应该用 in，只是当时没想起来。英文阅读的好处，又得一证。白居易《池上二首（一）》的最后英译，在如上译文的基础上，修改第五行的介词 with 为 in，虽然只是一个介词的改动，却对诗歌意境的提升起到了关键作用。

Over the Pond (No. 1 of two poems)　Bai Juyi

Sitting in the cool shade

　　of a bamboo grove, two

mountain monks are playing

　　chess. The chessboard is

checkered in sunlight

　　and bamboo shadow.

Screened by bamboos,

　　the players are unseeable;

only the sound of chessmen

　　is heard once in a great while.

（张智中　译）

（12）惜牡丹花（白居易）

惜牡丹花　白居易	**Peony Flowers**　Bai Juyi
惆怅阶前红牡丹， 晚来唯有两枝残。 明朝风起应吹尽， 夜惜衰红把火看。	Before stairs red peony flowers are melancholy; at dusk only two twigs bear some blossoms. The next morning a gale is to blow them off: with a torch I appreciate them this very night. （张智中　译）

读英文：

Where Gerald's snores were rhythmic and untroubled, into **the flickering light of an upheld candle**, her medicine-case under her arm, her hair smoothed neatly into place, and no button on her basque unlooped.

同时听到里面杰拉尔德平静而有节奏的鼾声；母亲让黑人手中的蜡烛照着，臂下挟着药品箱，头发已梳得熨熨贴贴，紧身上衣的钮扣也会扣好了。

在这句英文中，the flickering light of an upheld candle（手中蜡烛闪烁的光亮），正可用来英译"夜惜衰红把火看"所描写的摇曳之光。

《惜牡丹花》改译如下，并比较许渊冲的英译：

Peony Flowers　Bai Juyi Before the stairs red peony flowers are melancholy; at dusk only two twigs bear some blossoms. The next morning a gale is to blow them off: in the flickering light of an upheld candle, I admire them this very night. （张智中　译）	**The Last Look on the Peonies at Night**　Bai Juyi I'm saddened by the courtyard peonies brilliant red; At dusk only two of them are left on their bed. I am afraid they can't survive the morning blast; By lantern light I take a look, the long, long last.²² （许渊冲　译）

在许渊冲的译文中，为了押韵，第二行中添加了 bed（苗圃）。表面看来可以，但如果细思，苗圃，指的是培育树木幼株或农作物幼苗的基地。而让白居易感到惆怅的"阶前红牡丹"，不是苗圃中的牡丹幼苗。最后一行译文：By lantern light I take a look, the long, long last，造语生硬。译诗的语言应该自然流畅，是好的译诗的基本前提和保障。

（13）销夏（白居易）

白居易的《销夏》，一般读者可能很少见到，也很少英译。在每天坚持阅读英文的情况下，我们尝试给出如下英译。

销夏　白居易	**Summering**　Bai Juyi
何以销烦暑， 端居一院中。 眼前无长物，	How to pass the high summer when I am sitting in the courtyard enclosed with high walls?

22 许渊冲，唐诗三百首：汉英对照［Z］，北京：海豚出版社，2013：146。

窗下有清风。 热散由心静， 凉生为室空。 此时身自得， 难更与人同。	My eyes see nothing substantial to produce shade; a faint breeze, by the window, is fanning. A quiet mind dispels heat; an empty house enjoys the cool. Now I feel at ease, enjoying a carefree rest, which is a stranger to the rest of the world. （张智中　译）

原诗 8 行，译诗 11 行，原诗押韵，译诗自由无韵。不拘诗行不顾尾韵，虽为国内译者所恶，却吻合西方译诗潮流。

标题"销夏"的英译，采取 summer 的动词形式："过夏天，避暑"之意。因此，summering，简洁而形象。例如：

We summered in the mountains.

我们在山中避暑。

"何以销烦暑，端居一院中。"对应英文 How to pass the high summer when I am sitting in the courtyard enclosed with high walls? 汉语 2 行，英译 3 行出之，enclosed with high walls（高墙四围），乃深层之译，增补而出，强调"烦暑"之困扰。其中，形容词 high 重复，但语义略微不同，带来译诗的玩味之处。

"眼前无长物，窗下有清风。"对应英文 My eyes see nothing substantial to produce shade; a faint breeze, by the window, is fanning. 同样，汉语 2 行，英译 3 行。"无长物"在汉语中语义宽泛，相应的英文 nothing substantial to produce shade（没有什么可以遮阴的实物）走向了具体。"清风"，英译 a faint breeze ... is fanning，如此搭配，带来新鲜的语感，特别是 fanning（像扇子一样吹风），正描写了清风无计可销夏的微弱之风。另外，从音韵的角度而言, see, substantial 押头韵，shade, faint 押元音韵，faint, fanning 与 breeze, by 分别形成跨行头韵。如此音韵技法，在当代英诗中，远比尾韵更为常见。

"热散由心静，凉生为室空。"对应英文 A quiet mind dispels heat; an empty house enjoys the cool. 大体直译，采用陌生化搭配，取得良好效果。这里的 cool 为名词，前置定冠词，往往表示"凉爽，凉气"之意。例如：

We are enjoying the cool of the evening.

我们在纳晚凉。

"此时身自得，难更与人同。"对应 Now I feel at ease, enjoying a carefree

rest, which is a stranger to the rest of the world. 再次，汉语 2 行，英译 3 行出之。"身自得"之英译，用了 at ease 和 enjoying a carefree rest 两个短语，乃充分翻译。英语词典上例句：

Yaks are **enjoying a carefree rest** in the water.

牦牛在水中悠然自得。

随后的 a stranger to the rest of the world（世人对此陌生），可能对国内读者的理解带来挑战，但对于熟悉英语 -er 类词语妙用的读者来说，却会带来惊喜之感。另外，这里的两个 rest，词形相同，含义却异，也带来一定的语言审美效果。

（14）六月二十七日望湖楼醉书五绝（其一）（苏轼）

读到这样一个英文句子：

An endless bed of grey moved over the sky and land, bringing sheets of rain that smudged the colour and contours out of everything.

一层厚厚的乌云灰压压地盖住天地，一场又一场的豪雨几乎要将所有东西的颜色轮廓都打掉。

令人想起苏轼的这首诗：

六月二十七日望湖楼醉书五绝（其一）　苏轼

黑云翻墨未遮山，白雨跳珠乱入船。

卷地风来忽吹散，望湖楼下水如天。

Tipsy at Lake-view Pavilion　Su Shi

An endless bed of grey moves over the sky and mountain,

murky clouds churning like Chinese ink, which brings

sheets of rain that smudges the color and contours

out of everything, yet a distant hill has not been

completely screened from view. White rain-

drops bounce like pearls, beating the boat.

Gusts of earth-rolling wind scatter the

clouds, and the water of West Lake,

under the pavilion, stills and

is one with the sky.

（张智中　译）

译文中，an endless bed of grey moves over the sky and … which brings sheets of rain that smudges the color and contours out of everything，显然是对上引英文句子微调后的借用。遥想如果苏轼精通英文，或者是个一流的英文作家的话，他写出这样的诗句来，也当颇感自豪了。

比较许渊冲的译文：

Written While Drunken in Lake View Pavilion　Su Shi

Dark clouds like spilt ink spread over the mountains quiet;

Raindrops like bouncing pearls into the boat run riot.

A sudden rolling gale dispels clouds far and nigh;

Calmed water in the lake becomes one with the sky.[23]

（15）暮江吟（白居易）

见这样一个英文句子：

The sinking sun laid a red path from the horizon towards the shore.

西斜的太阳朝海平线划下一道红痕。

自然想起白居易的诗来：

暮江吟　*白居易*

一道残阳铺水中，半江瑟瑟半江红。

可怜九月初三夜，露似真珠月似弓。

A River at Sunset　Bai Juyi

The sinking sun lays a red path from the horizon

towards the river, lending a beam of light to

the water: half reddish and half greenish.

Loveable is the third night of the tenth

moon: dewdrops are pearls,

and the moon,

a bow.

（张智中　译）

把"一道残阳铺水中"英译为：The sinking sun lays a red path from the horizon

---

23 袁行霈编；徐放，韩珊今译；许渊冲英译，新编千家诗 [Z]，北京：中华书局，2006：113。

towards the river，境界恢弘壮观，与原诗诗意契合，语言给人美感。

虽然我们对此译文已经比较满意，后来还是读到了另一个英文句子：

> The moon shone high, and **cast a trembling copy of itself** over the deep water.

> 月亮很高、很明亮，在深不可测的海面投下颤抖着的影子。

这个句子，如果我们反复阅读，仔细品味，就会觉得是非常好的表达。尤其是 cast a trembling copy of itself（投下月亮自己那颤抖着的版本）。其实，这里的 copy，"拷贝"、"复制品"，非词典上的解释所能表达。多么富有诗意的想象和比喻。月亮如此，残阳呢，似可模仿。那么，再译《暮江吟》：

> **A River at Sunset**　Bai Juyi
> The sinking sun lays a red path from the horizon
> towards the river, casting a trembling copy
> of itself over the water: half reddish,
> half greenish. Loveable is the
> third night of the tenth moon:
> dewdrops are pearls,
> and the moon,
> a bow.
> （张智中　译）

以上两种译文，无论是 lending a beam of light to the water，还是 casting a trembling copy of itself over the water，都是地道的英文表达。

后来，竟然又读到两个与《暮江吟》相关的例子：

> The sun **poured its rays on** their backs.
> 阳光倾泻在他们的背上。

> In the autumn, **toward the close of day**, when the setting sun **shed a blood-red glow over** the western sky, and **the reflection of the crimson clouds tinged the whole river with red**, **brought** a glow **to** the faces of the two friends, and gilded the trees, whose leaves were already turning the first chill touch of winter.

> 秋天，白昼将尽时，夕阳将西边的天空照得血红，深红色云霞的倒影染红了整片河水，把两个朋友的脸照得通红，给树木镀上了

金色，树上的叶子刚触及冬的第一缕寒意便已经变了颜色。

这里，the sun poured its rays on …，toward the close of day，the setting sun shed a blood-red glow over …，the reflection of the crimson clouds tinged the whole river with red 等，似乎都是《暮江吟》的片段阐释。故此，散文英译如下：

> The sinking sun, toward the close of day, pours its rays on the river, over which it sheds a blood-red glow, the reflection of crimson clouds tinging half the river with red, the other half a deep blue. The sight brings boundless charm to the third night of the tenth moon: dewdrops are pearls, and the moon, a bow.

诗体排列如下：

A River at Sunset　Bai Juyi

The sinking sun, toward the close of day, pours its rays

on the river, over which it sheds a blood-red glow,

the reflection of crimson clouds tinging half

the river with red, the other half a deep

blue. The sight brings boundless

charm to the third night of the

tenth moon: dewdrops

are pearls, and

the moon,

a bow.

（张智中　译）

《暮江吟》，又一首散体英译之诗。如果不是借用英文表达，任何高明的译者，一般都很难译出如此精彩的句子来。美国翻译家葛浩文反复强调英文阅读的重要性，实在是翻译要诀之一了。

（16）崔兴宗写真咏（王维）

读到这么一个简单的英文句子：

The years went on, and Ernest **ceased to be a boy**.

岁月如梭，欧内斯特不再是少年。

想到王维的一首绝句及其英译：

崔兴宗写真咏　王维	**Ode to the Portrait of a Friend**　Wang Wei
画君少年时， 如今君已老。 今时新识人， 知君旧时好。	I painted you as a boy, and now you are an old man. I have made a host of friends: you are my friend of friends. （张智中　译）

于是，改译如下，首先散体：

I painted you as a boy and, as the years go on, you cease to be a boy. I have made a host of friends through all these years, and you are my friend of friends, now an old man.

诗体排列如下：

Ode to the Portrait of a Friend　Wang Wei

I painted you as a boy and, as the years

go on, you cease to be a boy. I

have made a host of friends

through all these years,

and you are my friend

of friends, now

an old man.

（张智中　译）

（17）戏答诸少年（白居易）

另外，上引英文句子：The years went on, and Ernest ceased to be a boy（岁月如梭，欧内斯特不再是少年），还可用于另外一首诗的改译：

戏答诸少年　白居易	**Replying the Youngsters in Jest**　Bai Juyi
顾我长年头似雪， 饶君壮岁气如云。 朱颜今日虽欺我， 白发他时不放君。	Taking advantage of me who is white-crowned, youngsters are in the prime of their life. Today, red faces bully me;

| | tomorrow, white hair
won't pardon you.
（张智中　译） |

又读到英文：...in his young playdays, ...（孩提时代。）

《戏答诸少年》改译如下：

Replying the Youngsters in Jest　　Bai Juyi

Taking advantage of me who is white-crowned,

youngsters are in the prime of their life.

Today, red faces, in their young play-

days, bully me; as the years go on,

they cease to be boys, and

the white hair won't

pardon them.

（张智中　　译）

（18）江行无题一百首（五）（钱珝）

读到这样两个英文句子：

The trees **are silvered with** hoar frost.

这些树木披着银霜。

They **are busying themselves in** packing up.

他们正忙着整理行装。

就想起一首唐诗及其英译：

江行无题一百首（五） 钱珝 万木已清霜， 江边村事忙。 故溪黄稻熟， 一夜梦中香。	**At the Riverside (No. 5 of one hundred poems)**　　Qian Xu A clear frost onto myriads of trees; busy is farming at riversides. Yellow paddy is ripe in native stream which, through- out the night, sweetens my dream. （张智中　译）

借鉴如上英文，改译如下：

At the Riverside (No. 5 of one hundred poems)   Qian Xu

Myriads of trees are silvered with hoar frost,

when farmers are busying themselves in

farming at riversides. The native

stream is golden with ripe

paddy which, throughout

the night, sweetens

my dream.

（张智中　译）

（19）小池（杨万里）

读英文：

I was able to spot **streams of tears silently escaping from the corners** of her eyes.

发现有一行泪水顺着舅母的眼角悄悄往下走。

表示落泪或"泪水往下走"，如果说 tears running down the corners of her eyes，就平淡多了。这里的 escaping，尤其形象。又读到另一个巧用 escaping 的英文句子：

The whole field was richly spread with grass and a variety of delicate flowers. But that which gave no less delight than any of the rest was **a small running stream**, descending from one of the valleys that divided two of the little hills, **escaping** through a crack in the center of a large boulder, murmuring as it dripped down into the stream, a most delightful sound to hear.

整片田野则是绿草如茵，繁花似锦。不过最叫她们开心的还是那条小溪，溪水从两座山之间的狭谷中流出来，穿越一块巨石中间的裂缝，当水滴滴入小溪之中时，会发出清脆悦耳的声音。

这里，a small running stream ...escaping ...，描写形象，生动入微。联想到杨万里那首有名的《小池》：

小池　杨万里

泉眼无声惜细流，树阴照水爱晴柔。

小荷才露尖尖角，早有蜻蜓立上头。
尝试英译：

A Small Pond   Yang Wanli

Trickling streams of water are

　　silently and cautiously escaping

from the eye of the fountain;

　　the reflected shadows of trees

on water love zephyr in days fine.

　　A tender lotus leaf is cutting a fine

figure above water, when a playful

　　dragonfly flies to settle on it.

（张智中　译）

有了 escaping 的妙用，译文终于多了点回味的余地。

（20）从军北征（李益）

有时，我们读到一个英文句子，联想到翻译过的某一首古诗，便可改进译文。例如：

　　… so amply does the sun bathe heaven with radiance, that it would sparkle like a point of light for us. **The village was dotted with people with their heads in air**; and the children were in a bustle all along the street and far up the straight road that climbs the hill, where we could still see them running in loose knots.

　　但是由于阳光普照天空，以至于在我们看来它也成了闪闪发光的了。村里到处有人抬头仰望，孩子们成群地在街上跑，跑上远处直通山顶的道路，我们可以看见他们在那条小路上三三两两地奔跑着。

这里，The village was dotted with people with their heads in air（村里到处有人抬头仰望），令人想起唐代一首边塞诗：

从军北征　李益

天山雪后海风寒，横笛偏吹行路难。

碛里征人三十万，一时回首月中看。

及其英译：

原　译	改　译
Marching in the Moonlight　Li Yi The sea wind blows chilly after snowing in Heavenly Mountain. The fluting of *Hard Is the Way*, overflowing with sorrow, at which three hundred thousand soldiers walking in the desert, all lift eyes toward the bright moon: reduced to home- sickness. （张智中　译）	**Marching in the Moonlight**　Li Yi The sea wind blows chilly after snowing in Heavenly Mountain. The fluting of *Hard Is the Way*, overflowing with sorrow, at which three hundred thousand soldiers, dotting the desert with their heads in air, all lift eyes toward the bright moon: reduced to home- sickness. （张智中　译）

原译中，walking in the desert，措语平淡，改译 dotting the desert with their heads in air，生动传神，画面感极强。

（21）独坐敬亭山（李白）

在上引英文句子中，the straight road that climbs the hill（直通山顶的道路），这里的 climbs，也很有诗意。又读到另两个巧用 climb 的英文句子：

After completing the punishment, however, I will **climb to Heaven**.

惩罚过后，我会去天堂。

To the east the night had cracked open, revealing a pale band of light that began **to climb and fill the sky**.

东方的夜空已经破晓，露出一道苍白的光，越来越高，最后布满整个天空。

平时我们不太注意的 climb，在英文中却有如此诗意之用。自然想起一首名诗及其英译：

独坐敬亭山　李白

众鸟高飞尽，孤云独去闲。

相看两不厌，只有敬亭山。

原 译	改 译
Sitting Alone in Jingting Mountain Li Bai A bevy of birds are gone, one and all; the lonely cloud is wafting alone, at ease. I never weary of Jingting Mountain, which is my favorite kind of scenery, and the mountain, never weary of me. （张智中　译）	**Sitting Alone in Jingting Mountain** Li Bai A bevy of birds climb the sky of skies, to be gone, one and all; the lonely cloud is wafting at ease, alone. I never weary of Jingting Mountain, which is my favorite kind of scenery, and the mountain, never weary of me. （张智中　译）

改译后的 A bevy of birds climb the sky of skies，不仅动词 climb 用得好，而且 the sky of skies，正可绘九重天之高远。译文显有进步。

（22）后宫词（白居易）

有时，英文里的一个非常普通的单词，如果用在古诗英译里，也可起到妙不可言的作用。例如：

She often sat next this pot, sighing or weeping for her lost love. Day by day, **this was her only activity**, to the great astonishment of her brothers and many other friends.

她终日陪着这个罐子，为失去的爱情伤感落泪。日复一日，每天如此，这情形让她的兄长们、朋友们都大为吃惊。

这个句子中，this was her only activity（每天如此），看起来简单，但却深有余味，初学英文者可能认识这些单词，但却不能体会其造语之妙。再如下面句子中的 activities，也颇堪回味：

Now we can devote more hours to **activities** that can genuinely increase our happiness.

来看白居易的这首诗及其英译：

后宫词　白居易

泪湿罗巾梦不成，夜深前殿按歌声。

红颜未老恩先断，斜倚熏笼坐到明。

原　译	改　译
Poem of Rear Palace　Bai Juyi Tears moistening the towel without a fond dream; deep into night the temple is aloud with singing. Before fair faces fade no favor is granted; leaning against a heating cage till it dawns. 　　（张智中　译）	**Poem of Rear Palace**　Bai Juyi Tears moistening the towel without a fond dream; deep into night the temple is aloud with singing. Before fair faces fade no favor is granted; leaning against a heating cage, night by night, their only activity, till it dawns. 　　（张智中　译）

　　将英文的 day by day，改成 night by night，另添补充短语 their only activity（她们唯一的每个晚上的活动），就把宫女的寂寞尽写出来。如果不读英文，谁能想起 their only activity 这样的措词呢，虽然这是极其简单平实的用语。

（23）宫词（朱庆余）

　　又一首闺怨诗：

　　　　宫词　朱庆余

　　　　寂寂花时闭院门，美人相并立琼轩。

　　　　含情欲说宫中事，鹦鹉前头不敢言。

原　译	改　译
A Palace Poem　Zhu Qingyu In flowery season the lonely gate is closed; beauties stand together against the balustrade. On the verge of talking about palace affairs, they dare not speak before the parrot. 　　（张智中　译）	**A Palace Poem**　Zhu Qingyu In flowery season the lonely gate is closed; beauties, who have had their share of beauty, stand together against the balustrade. On the verge of talking about palace affairs, words rising to their lips are taken back — they dare not speak before the parrot. 　　（张智中　译）

改译中，添加了一个定语从句：who have had their share of beauty，来限定其前的名词 beauties。这一改动，来自英文阅读：

I have had my share of beauty.

毕竟，我也曾漂亮过。

原诗字面上没有这样的意思，但是，添加之后，可增进原诗所要表达的意思，与上一首"红颜未老恩先断"有类似之感慨。因此，当属于合理添加。而且，表示抽象意义的 beauty，与之前表示具体美人的 beauties，形成同源词语，具修辞效果。

另外，改译中还添加了一个短句：words rising to their lips are taken back，这也借鉴自英文名著《飘》（*Gone with the Wind*）中的一个句子：

But automatically, **the words** Ellen had taught her to say in such emergencies **rose to her lips** and casting down her eyes, from force of long habit, she murmured.

不过，母亲教导她在这种场合应当说的那些话自然而然溜到了嘴边，于是她出于长期养成的习惯，把眼睛默默地向下望，然后低声说。

这里，words rose to her lips（话到嘴边），非常形象。欲言又止，及时收回了想说的话。英文：I take back my words（我收回我说的话。）两者合并，成为：words rising to their lips are taken back（到了嘴边的话又收回了。）这样英译"鹦鹉前头不敢言"，可谓形象。

后来，又读菲茨杰拉德（Fitzgerald）名著 *The Great Gatsby* 中如下两个英文句子：

It was **on the tip of my tongue to** ask his name when Jordan looked around and smiled.

我都准备问他的名字了，这时乔丹回头对我笑了笑。

A little overwhelmed, I began **the generalized evasions** which that question deserves.

我有些手足无措，闪烁其词地糊弄了几句。

这里，on the tip of my tongue to 表示欲言又止，the generalized evasions 表示闪烁其词或含糊其辞，正可描写"鹦鹉前头不敢言"之状貌。

《宫词》另译如下，并回译汉语：

A Palace Poem Zhu Qingyu	宫中之诗 朱庆余
In flowery season the lonely gate is closed, which finds beauties stand against the balustrade. On the verge of talking about palace affairs — it was on the tip of their tongue to talk, before the parrot, they dare not speak — only generalized evasions. （张智中　译）	花季，孤独之门紧闭，美人并肩依阑干。宫廷之事——欲言，舌尖婉转：鹦鹉前，如何言？——其词烁而闪。 （张智中　译）

我们不妨比较一下许渊冲的英译，并回译以观效果：

Within the Palace Zhu Qingyu	宫廷之内 朱庆余
The palace gate is closed, even flowers feel lonely; Fair maidens side by side in shade of arbour stand. They will complain of their lonesome palace life, only Afraid the parrot might tell a tale secondhand.[24]	大门紧闭，宫花也感到寂寞，美丽的女孩并肩站在凉亭下；想要抱怨其孤独的宫廷生活：担心鹦鹉搬弄是非到处传话。 （张智中　译）

显然，不同的翻译风格。

（24）与浩初上人同看山寄京华亲故（柳宗元）

读到如下英文句子：

And on each of them stood a little palace, **shaped in the fashion of castles**.

每座小山的山顶上都有一栋别墅，看上去很像一座座城堡。

如果逆向思维，把这句汉语当做原文，英文当做译文的话，"看上去很像"，有哪个译者，包括英美译者，能想起来用 shaped in the fashion of 这样的表达呢？越想，越觉得这种表达巧妙。同样，可用来英译唐诗：

与浩初上人同看山寄京华亲故　柳宗元

海畔尖山似剑芒，秋来处处割愁肠。

若为化作身千亿，散向峰头望故乡。

---

24 许渊冲，唐诗三百首：汉英对照［Z］，北京：海豚出版社，2013：187。

原　译	改　译
A Mountain View　Liu Zongyuan Blade-like are sea-side pinnacles, which cut the heart when fall comes. If transformed into millions of bodies, I would stand from top to top to gaze homeward. （张智中　译）	**A Mountain View**　Liu Zongyuan Sea-side pinnacles are shaped in the fashion of swords, which cut the heart when fall comes. If transformed into millions of bodies, I would stand from top to top　—　to gaze homeward. （张智中　译）

　　首句"海畔尖山似剑芒"，原译 Blade-like are sea-side pinnacles，只是平实之译，改译 Sea-side pinnacles are shaped in the fashion of swords，变成厚道之英文，语言可堪玩味。

　　另外，又读到美国诗人 Rupi Kaur 2017 年在 Andrews McMeel Publishing 出版社出版的诗集 *The Sun and Her Flowers*，其中有如下几行：

> **i shattered into a million little pieces**
>
> and those pieces shattered into a million more
>
> crumbled into dust till
>
> there was nothing left of me but the silence

又读到如下含有动词 collapse 的英文句子：

　　Melly **collapsed** into tears and laid her head on the pillow.

　　Had Melanie not been so faint, so sick, so heartsore, she would have **collapsed** at his question.

　　When she found him one day standing on his head in Melanie's bed and saw him **collapse** on her, she slapped him.

　　It did not occur to her that Ellen could not have foreseen the **collapse** of the civilization in which she raised her daughters, could not have anticipated the disappearing of the places in society for which she trained them so well.

　　His old black face was as pitiful as a child's under its mother's disapproval, his dignity **collapsed**.

　　After the complete moral **collapse** which had sent her to Atlanta and to Rhett, the appropriation of her sister's betrothed seemed a minor affair and one not to be bothered with at this time.

"The Yankees coming here?" cried Pitty and, her small feet turning under her, she **collapsed** on the sofa, too frightened for tears.

英文名著《飘》（*Gone with the Wind*）里的一个句子：

Maybelle **collapsed** with blushes against Fanny's shoulder and the two girls hid their faces in each other's necks and giggled, as other voices began calling other names, other amounts of money.

梅贝尔刷地脸一下红了，赶紧伏在范妮的肩上，两个人交缠着脖子把脸藏起来，吃吃地笑着，这时有许多别的声音在喊着别人的名字，提出不同的价额。

借鉴如上英文，《与浩初上人同看山寄京华亲故》改译如下：

A Mountain-Scape　Liu Zongyuan

Sea-side

pinnacles are

shaped in the fashion

of swords, which cut my heart

when fall comes. Bleeding inwardly,

I collapse into a million little pieces, to be

scattered from top to top — to gaze homeward.

（张智中　译）

比较孙大雨的译文：

On Sighting the Mounts with Bonze Haochu, Lines Written to My Kin and Friends in the Capital　Liu Zongyuan

Shrill, seaside peaks like poniards pointing skywards

In this fall day everywhere my sad bowels pierce.

How could I be turned into a million selves

To be scattered on to those tops to descry my homeland?[25]

柳宗元《与浩初上人同看山寄京华亲故》译文中的 fashion 一词，笔者还

---

25 孙大雨，英译唐诗选：汉英对照［Z］，上海：上海外语教育出版社，2007：303。

读到另一处妙用：

春雪　韩愈	**Snow in Spring**　Han Yu
新年都未有芳华，	The new year has yet no fragrant blossoms,
二月初惊见草芽。	But the second moon suddenly sees the grass sprouting;
白雪却嫌春色晚，	The white snow, vexed by the late coming of spring's colours,
故穿庭树作飞花。	Of set purpose darts among the courtyard's trees to fashion flying petals.
	（Robert Kotewell & Norman Smith　译）

这里的 fashion，做动词用，"制作；使成形；把……塑造成"之意。例如，fashion a canoe from a tree trunk（用树干制成独木舟。）所以，这里 to fashion flying petals，意即"呈现飞花之状"。如此措词，一般中国译者很难想到。

（25）山行（杜牧）

阅读英文小说，见到这样一个句子：

The wood stopped here, and **their eyes were instantly caught by** Pemberley House.

林地就到此为止，即刻映入眼帘的就是彭贝利庄园。

"映入眼帘"，汉语常见，相应的英文 their eyes were instantly caught by 很少见到，但却不乏诗味。杜牧这首有名的《山行》：

山行　杜牧

远上寒山石径斜，白云深处有人家。

停车坐爱枫林晚，霜叶红于二月花。

原　译	改　译
A Mountain Trip　Du Mu	**A Mountain Trip**　Du Mu
A circuitous rocky path	A circuitous rocky path leads
leads to a cold mountain;	to a cold mountain; in depth
in depth of white clouds,	of white clouds, my eyes
there are a few households.	are caught by a household.
I stop my coach to appreciate	I stop my coach to admire
eventide maple woods:	eventide maple woods:
frost-bitten leaves are redder	frost-bitten leaves are redder
than March flowers.	than March flowers.
（张智中　译）	（张智中　译）

"有人家"，原译 there are a few households，原文平淡，译文平淡，似乎也只能这样了。改译：my eyes are caught by a household，模拟上引英文句子而来，译文鲜活起来。另外，"白云深处"之"人家"，似不可多，因改单数。

晨读英文：

For a considerable portion of the way there are no houses lying near the road, and, there is one **residence**, some way from the road, so secluded that no other house lies within a mile of it by land.

沿路很少有人家，倒是离路稍远的地方有一处独门独户的院落，而方圆一英里之内便再没有别的人家了。

The villages **straggle** in the mountains.
村庄散布在山林之中。

It was difficult to **clamber** the mountain.
爬上那座大山是困难的。

The **eventide** is calling me to take a look into your eyes.
黄昏在召唤我注视你的双眼。

汲取如上英文表达，杜牧《山行》可英译如下：

A Mountain Trip   Du Mu

A winding path leads upward,
    heavenward, for a considerable
        portion of which there are
no houses lying near the road
    except straggling stones, until
        I clamber to the cold mountain-
top, to find a lofty residence
    in the clouds of clouds. I stop
        my coach to admire eventide
maple woods: frost-bitten
    leaves are redder, redder than
        flowers of the third moon.

（张智中　译）

（26）咏柳（贺知章）

读到霍克斯英译《红楼梦》第八回中的一个句子：

> 李嬷嬷听了，又是急，又是笑，说道："真真这林姐儿，说出一句话来，比刀子还利害。"

> Nannie Li did not know whether to feel upset or amused. 'Really, Miss Lin. Some of the things you say **cut sharper than a knife**!'

就想起贺知章的名句："二月春风似剪刀"，及其英译：

咏柳　贺知章	Ode to Willows　He Zhizhang
碧玉妆成一树高， 万条垂下绿丝绦。 不知细叶谁裁出， 二月春风似剪刀。	Emerald jade decorated into the height of a tree; thousands of twigs drooping with green silk braids. O who has tailored so many fine willow leaves? The spring wind of March is like a pair of scissors. （张智中　译）

英译：The spring wind of March is like a pair of scissors，与原文贴近，但语言平淡。借用霍克斯的佳译，似可改译如下：The spring wind of March cuts sharper than a pair of scissors。这样一来，意象更加鲜明了。全诗改译如下：

Ode to Willows　He Zhizhang

Emerald jade is decorated

　　into the height of a tall tree;

thousands of twigs are drooping

　　with green silk braids. Who

has tailored so many fine

　　willow leaves? The spring

wind of March cuts sharper

　　than a pair of scissors.

（张智中　译）

（27）金缕衣（杜秋娘）

> 劝君莫惜金缕衣，劝君惜取少年时。
>
> 有花堪折直须折，莫待无花空折枝。

原　译	改　译
Golden Clothes　Du Qiuniang I urge you to cherish your bloom of youth instead of golden clothes. Pluck blossoming flowers now, no tarry: only bare boughs barely stay. （张智中　译）	**Golden Clothes**　Du Qiuniang I urge you to cherish your bloom of youth instead of golden clothes. Pluck off blossoming flowers now, no tarry: only bare boughs barely stay. （张智中　译）

改译中，除了诗行缩进之外，只是在动词 pluck 的后面添加了一个副词 off，这样似乎更加形象。英文句子：

Plucking off branches, she made an honorable crown.

她摘下多个枝条，编了一顶光荣的桂冠。

如果不是读到这样的英文句子，我们会觉得 pluck 就行，不会想起来添加副词 off。

（28）近试上张水部（朱庆余）

读到这样几个英文句子：

Mr. Lorry **asked him in a whisper**, with a little anger.

罗瑞先生有些生气，轻声质问道。

"You will go south?" said Gerald, **a little ring of uneasiness in his voice**.

"去南方吗？"杰拉德有点不安地问。

这里的英文表述 a little ring of uneasiness in his voice，很是生动微妙，令人想到"妆罢低声问夫婿"。又读到这样一个句子：

His dark **brows** and all his **lines**, **were finely drawn**.

他的黑眉毛和其他线条倒是生得很好看。

又想到"画眉深浅入时无？"于是，尝试英译朱庆余的诗：

近试上张水部　朱庆余

洞房昨夜停红烛，待晓堂前拜舅姑。

妆罢低声问夫婿：画眉深浅入时无？

原　译	改　译
To an Official When the Test Approaches Zhu Qingyu In the bridal chamber a red candle burns throughout the night; in the morning I will pay respects to my parents-in-law. After making up I ask my husband in whisper: do I pencil my eyebrows nicely? （张智中　译）	**To an Official When the Test Approaches** Zhu Qingyu In the bridal chamber a red candle burns throughout the night; in the morning I will pay respects to my parents-in- law. After making up I ask my husband in a whisper, a little ring of uneasiness in my voice: my brows and all my lines, are they finely drawn? （张智中　译）

改译添加了短语 a little ring of uneasiness in my voice（我的语气中带着不安），从而译出了原诗所暗示的口气。

后来，又读到一些英文句子：

Our final test **is around the corner**.

我们的期末测试即将来临。

He spoke **in a subdued voice**.

他压低了声音说。

The shrieks and the cries were **audible** there, though subdued by the distance.

虽然距离很远，但那尖叫在这儿也还隐约可闻。

This dialogue had been held in so very low a whisper, that **not a word of it had reached the young lady's ears**.

他们是在窃窃私语中进行的这番对话，没有一个字传到那位小姐的耳中。

这些也可用来英译"妆罢低声问夫婿"之"低声"。

《近试上张水部》另译如下：

To an Official When the Test Is Around the Corner　Zhu Qingyu

Last night sees the bridal

　　chamber bright with

　　　a red candle, which

keeps burning throughout

　　the night; in the morning

　　　I pay respects to my

parents-in-law. After

　　making-up I ask my husband

　　　in a subdued voice, barely

audible, to reach his ears:

　　"my brows and lines,

　　　are they penciled nicely?"

（张智中　译）

（29）逢雪宿芙蓉山主人（刘长卿）

日暮苍山远，天寒白屋贫。

柴门闻犬吠，风雪夜归人。

原　　译	改　　译
Lodging at the Home of Host of Lotus Hill for the Snowy Night　Liu Changqing At sundown the bleak hill looms afar; under the cold sky a white cottage is poor. The wicket door hears a dog barking: against winds & snows a night arrival. （张智中　译）	**Lodging at the Home of Lotus Hill Host in a Snowy Night**　Liu Changqing At sundown the pale hill looms from afar; beneath the cold sky, a cottage, silvery thatched, is melting into the shadowy background of a faint landscape, a mere dot on the horizon, which looks homey and inviting. From the wicket door travels the sound of a dog yelping at the approaching of a night arrival against winds and snows. （张智中　译）

有多处改译。其中，a cottage, silvery thatched, is melting into the shadowy background of a faint landscape，源自 Miss Read 英文小说 *Tyler's Row* 中的一个句子：

> Holding the cool stalks of the mint, she looked at their home. There it stood, as it had done for generations, **silvery thatched**, ancient and snug, **melting into the shadowy background of** trees and downland.

随后的 a mere dot on the horizon，来自英文句子：

> The ship became **a mere dot on the horizon**.
>
> 轮船在地平线上成了一个小黑点。

接下来，which looks homey and inviting，是受到如下英文句子的启发：

> There was an old house, two stories, that **looked homey and inviting**.
>
> 面前是一座房子，两层楼，看上去既温馨又吸引人。

是啊，"既温馨又吸引人"，不正是苍山风雪中"白屋"的形象吗？可以说，人生无处不"天寒"，人人不富只觉"贫"；花花世界耀花眼，终极色彩乃是白。因此，读过此诗的人，应该一辈子都不会忘记刘长卿诗中的"白屋"。其实，"天寒白屋贫"之"白屋"，像极了人生之灯塔，具有温情归宿之象征意义。因此，用英文形容词 homey 和 inviting 来译之，正是译出了原诗的深层含义，是"天寒白屋贫"的当代阐释。

后面的 the sound of a dog yelping，来自这个英文句子：

> There is **the sound of a dog yelping**.
>
> 这时传来一只狗的叫声。

《逢雪宿芙蓉山主人》，笔者的另一个散文英译：

A Night Arrival to the Cottage　Liu Changqing

Sundown, bleak hills remote; a white cottage, wretched and forlorn, is sheltered under cold heavens. When I, with persistent determination, slowly and steadily approach the door by dragging my weary body, I hear the barking, in soothing accents, of a dog, which abruptly breaks the enveloping sheet of silence, while swelling melodiously in the fresh air before dying away into the snowstorm from which I am on the point of disengaging myself — to be a night arrival.

回译汉语：

日落，苍凉之山遥远；一个白色的小屋，怜兮孤兮，庇护在寒冷的天宇之下。当我——意决而志坚、缓慢而孤注地拖着疲惫的身躯——接近屋门之时，我听见了犬吠之声，慰藉的音符，突然打破了四周八围帐幔也似的沉寂——在清清冷冷的空气中，婉婉转转，悠悠扬扬，直至消失在暴风雪中——我正从中脱身，成为这苍茫夜色中的一个归客。

虽然散文而冗长，却不失浓郁之诗意。英译中，有多处英文借用。例如 heavens，借鉴自如下英文：

In the distance the **heavens** were red from the glow of a volcano.

远方，天空被火山的光亮映得通红。

Persistent，借鉴自如下英文：

Johnny smiled patiently, and his mother was aware of a distinct shock at the **persistent** absence of his peevishness and irritability.

约翰尼耐心地笑了笑，母亲看到他这样始终不发怒也不闹别扭，觉得更吃惊了。

Dragging my weary body，借鉴自如下两个英文句子：

She tried to **drag herself** out of Liza's clutches.

她想要从莉莎的手中挣开。

After supper I exhibited the same marks of languor as on the preceding evening; but this time, as I yielded to fatigue, or as if I had become familiarized with danger, I **dragged myself toward** my bed, let my robe fall, and lay down.

晚饭过后，我装出和前一天晚上相同的倦怠的样子。但这一次，好像我不胜疲惫，或是仿佛自己已经熟悉了这种危险，我拖着身体走到床边，让身上的长袍落下，顺势躺在床上。

In soothing accents，借鉴自如下英文：

Some turn in the road, some new object suddenly perceived and recognized, reminded me of days gone by, and were associated with the lighthearted gaiety of boyhood. The very winds whispered **in soothing accents**, and maternal Nature bade me weep no more.

　　路上的某个转弯处，某个新东西会突然映入眼帘，让我想起逝去的岁月，联想起儿时无忧无虑的快乐。和风在低声细语，大自然母亲哄我入睡。

表示声音的动词 swelling，可见于如下英文句子：

The room is crowded with men, shouting, cursing, laughing, singing — a confused, inchoate uproar **swelling** into a sort of unity, a meaning — the bewildered, furious, baffled defiance of a beast in a cage. Nearly all the men are drunk. Many bottles are passed from hand to hand.

　　房间里挤满了人，他们叫呀、骂呀、笑呀、唱呀——混乱而模糊的骚动声渐渐高涨，之后变得整齐一致而意味深长——就像笼中困兽那猛烈而无奈的反抗。几乎所有的人都喝醉了。人们依次传着一瓶瓶酒。

再看这个句子：

She sang, and her voice flowed in a rich cadence, **swelling** or **dying away** like a nightingale of the woods.

　　她唱起了歌，歌声婉转悠扬，就像树林里的夜莺。

不仅有 swelling，还有其反义词语 dying away，从而为《逢雪宿芙蓉山主人》的英译提供了支撑：while swelling melodiously in the fresh air before dying away into the snowstorm。

至于 I am on the point of disengaging myself，可见如下四个英文句子：

They had not as yet had any unpleasant encounters, and the journey seemed **on the point of** being successfully accomplished, when the elephant, becoming restless, suddenly stopped.

　　他们还没有碰到任何烦恼的事情，旅程似乎能够顺利地完成了。就在这时，大象变得焦躁不安，突然停了下来。

He was **on the point of** making loose his skiff to return homewards, when he saw a light gleaming along the water from a distance, which seemed rapidly approaching.

他正要解开他的小船回家的时候，突然看见一道光在远处水面闪现，似乎在迅速靠近。

At this remark, Ardan pushed up his shock of red hair; he saw that he was **on the point of** being involved in a struggle with this person upon the very gist of the whole question. He looked sternly at him in his turn and said.

听到这里，阿当红色的头发都竖起来了，他意识到要和这个人在最关键的问题上争个你死我活了。他也虎视眈眈地望着对方，回敬道。

He managed **to disengage himself from** the contract.

他成功地为自己解除了契约义务。

最后，enveloping sheet of silence 中的 sheet，一般译者很难想到。其实，这个单词是在大量阅读英文的情况下，才得其妙用的。一般英汉词典上对 sheet 的定义，首先是名词，"被单；纸；一片"之意。下面三个句子中，sheet 不难理解。

Footsteps were easily printed on the snow! But soon, under a new **sheet**, every imprint would be effaced.

雪地上很容易留下脚印！但那些脚印很快就会被新下的雪覆盖。

Think how surprised everyone was when, on raising the **sheets**, they discovered Pinocchio half melted in tears!

大家把被单掀开，看见匹诺曹已哭成泪人的时候，想想他们是多么地惊奇！

The weather had changed back, a great wind was abroad, and beneath the lamp, in my room, with Flora at peace beside me, I sat for a long time before a blank **sheet** of paper and listened to the lash of the rain and the batter of the gusts.

天气变得又跟往常一样，屋外刮着大风。在我房间的灯下，弗洛拉在我旁边静静地睡着。我对着这张白纸坐了很久，倾听着大雨的拍打声和狂风的呼啸声。

但是，sheet 有时却有更加富有诗意的使用，词义虽简单，在英文中却有一般人想不到的妙用。例如：

The rain fell **in sheets**.

大雨滂沱。

Vivid flashes of lightning dazzled my eyes, illuminating the lake, making it appear like **a vast sheet of fire**.

耀眼的闪电让我目眩，闪电照亮了湖水，使它看上去像是一片火海。

A terrible sheet of lightning burst before their eyes, illuminating the dark day, and the thunder rolled wildly about them.

一道恐怖的闪电在他们眼前一闪，照亮了黑暗的天空，紧接着就是一阵轰轰隆隆的、发疯般的雷鸣。

My acquaintance with **sheets of water** was small, and the pool of Bly, at all events on the few occasions of my consenting, under the protection of my pupils, to affront its surface in the old flat-bottomed boat moored there for our use, had impressed me both with its extent and its agitation.

我对水域没有多少了解，而布莱的这片水，无论如何，在极少数我同意并有我学生们的保护的情况下，我们会划着一条泊在那里供我们使用的旧平底船打破水面的平静，宽广的水面、振荡的湖水给我留下了深刻印象。

And the four friends, seconded by Grimaud, pushed with the barrels of their muskets **an enormous sheet of the wall**, which bent as if pushed by the wind, and detaching itself from its base, fell with a horrible crash into the ditch.

于是四个朋友加上格里莫，一起用枪管推那堵巨大的墙。墙倾斜了，像被风吹了一样，从根部断裂开来，随着一声巨响倒在了壕沟里。

The river wound among low hills, so that sometimes the sun was at our backs, and sometimes it stood right ahead, and the river before us was

one sheet of intolerable glory.

河流绕着一座座矮山蜿蜒而行，因此，太阳时而照在我们身后，时而悬挂在我们正前方，而眼前的河流也呈现一片耀眼的光辉。

这些句子，因为有了 sheet 的使用，值得反复品味。名词之外，sheet 还可用作动词，"使成大片"之意。例如：sheeted rain：大雨。用 sheeted rain 表示大雨，同样是富有诗意的表达。再看下面句子中动词 sheet 的妙用：

But the air was mostly water, what with flying spray and **sheeted rain** that poured along at right angles to the perpendicular.

但是，因为飞溅的浪花和横扫而来的雨，空气中大部分都是海水。

The tropic rain **sheeted about them** so that they could see only the beach under their feet and the spiteful little waves from the lagoon that snapped and bit at the sand.

热带的骤雨遮住了他们的四周，他们只能看见脚底下的沙滩和吞噬着沙滩的凶狠的环礁湖小浪。

好了，关于刘长卿《逢雪宿芙蓉山主人》的散文英译，英文例子援引不少了。如果我们将其做诗行分割，可得自由体译诗如下，并回译汉语：

A Night Arrival to the Cottage Liu Changqing Sundown, bleak hills remote; a white cottage, wretched and forlorn, is sheltered under cold heavens. When I, with persistent determination, slowly and steadily approach the door by dragging my weary body, I hear the barking, in soothing accents, of a dog, which abruptly breaks the enveloping sheet of silence, while swelling melodiously in the fresh air before dying away into the snowstorm from which I am on the point of disengaging myself — to be a night arrival. （张智中　译）	白屋夜归人　刘长卿 日落，苍凉之山遥远；一个 白色的小屋，怜兮孤兮，庇护 在寒冷的天宇之下。当我 ——意决而志坚、缓慢 而孤注地拖着疲惫的身躯 ——接近屋门之时，我听见了 犬吠之声，慰藉的音符，突然 打破了四周八围帐幔也似的沉寂 ——在清清冷冷的空气中， 婉婉转转，悠悠扬扬，直至消失 在暴风雪中——我正从中脱身， 成为这苍茫夜色中的一个归客。 （张智中　译）

比较另外两种英译：

Seeking Shelter in Lotus Hill on a Snowy Night Liu Changqing	Staying with the Recluse of Mt. Hibiscus on a Snowy Night Liu Changqing
At sunset hillside village still seems far;	In the setting sun, dark hill seems distant;
Cold and deserted the thatched cottages are.	Stark thatched hut looks chilly and white.
At wicket gate a dog is heard to bark;	A dog is heard to bark at the bushwood gate;
With wind and snow I come when night is dark.	Someone is back on this windy, snowy night late.
（许渊冲　译）[26]	（都森、陈玉筠　译）[27]

格律体试图模拟原诗的音韵与诗形，结果往往因韵钳义，导致表层之译。

（30）悯农（一）（李绅）

　　锄禾日当午，汗滴禾下土。

　　谁知盘中餐，粒粒皆辛苦。

原　译	改　译
Poor Farmers (No. 1)　Li Shen	**Poor Farmers (No. 1)**　Li Shen
weed under the scorching	weed in the heat of the scorching summer sun,
sun, their sweat dripping	perspiration running down them in
& dropping. The rice	drops, dripping and dropping.
in the bowls, who knows,	The rice in the bowls, who
is the product	knows, is the product
of toiling	of toiling and
& moiling.	moiling.
（张智中　译）	（张智中　译）

　　译诗采用了跨题，即诗歌标题是主语。那么，译诗第一行的第一个动词 weed，便是谓语。不懂跨题者，一般很难读懂译诗。跨题虽不如跨行常见，却更具诗歌之美学效果。

　　改译中，in the heat of the scorching summer sun 源自两个英文句子：

　　The two men stood quite still **in the heat**, watching.

　　这两个男人在阳光下伫立着凝视这边。

　　这里的 in the heat，指的是 in the heat of the sun。

---

26 许渊冲，唐诗三百首：汉英对照［Z］，北京：海豚出版社，2013：75。

27 都森、陈玉筠，古韵新声——唐诗绝句 108 首（英汉对照）［Z］，武汉：华中科技大学出版社，2011：27。

... whether under **the scorching summer sun** or in pouring rain.

这里，the scorching summer sun，头韵的运用，非常之好。

后来，又读到这个英文句子：

Harold walked **under the heat of the sun**, the pelting of the rain, and the blue cold of the moon.

日晒雨淋，夜以继日，哈罗德不停地走。

那么，改译中 weed in the heat of the scorching summer sun，其中介词 in，也可以用 under。

改译的 perspiration running down them in drops，源自这个英文句子：

Perspiration ran down him in drops, his neck was all wet.

他汗如雨下，把脖子也都弄湿了。

改译之后不久，又读到英文句子：

For some time he lay without movement, **the genial sunshine pouring upon him and saturating his miserable body with its warmth.**

他一动不动地躺了一段时间，温和的阳光照在他身上。

这里的描写很形象，似可增译李绅之诗。于是，再次改译：

Poor Farmers (No. 1)   Li Shen

weed in the heat of the scorching summer sun,

sunlight pouring upon them and saturating

their miserable bodies with its heat.

Perspiration are running down

them in drops, dripping and

dropping. The rice in the

bowls, who knows,

is the product of

toiling and

moiling.

（张智中　译）

添译：sunlight pouring upon them and saturating their miserable bodies with its heat（阳光倾泻在他们身上，他们可怜的身体，被热气所浸透。）

又读到一个英文句子：

And the pale, flawless **skin gleamed with sweat**.

黯淡而又光滑的皮肤上闪着汗光。

若用上此句，可产生鲜明之意象。再次改译：

Poor Farmers (No. 1)   Li Shen

weed in the heat of the scorching summer sun,

sunlight pouring upon them and saturating

their miserable bodies with its heat,

which gleam with sweat gliding

down in drops, dripping and

dropping. The rice in the

bowls, who knows,

is the product of

toiling and

moiling.

（张智中　译）

改译中，用 bodies … gleam with sweat gliding，不仅意象鲜明，而且 gleam 与 gliding 押头韵，效果很好。后来，读到英文句子：

This book is **the product of** three authors.

其中的 product，印证了译文中 product 的合理性。

比较许渊冲的英译：

The Peasants (II)   Li Shen

At noon they weed with hoes;

Their sweat drips on soil.

Each bowl of rice, who knows?

Is the fruit of hard toil.

（许渊冲　译）[28]

其中，第二行中的介词 on，应该用 into，才比较形象。例如英文小说里类似的句子：

---

28 许渊冲，唐诗三百首：汉英对照［Z］，北京：海豚出版社，2013：159。

Tears are falling one by one from his closed eyes into soil around the plant.

比较之下，就知道借鉴英文表达，译诗语言就形象多了。

（31）渡江汉（宋之问）

渡汉江　宋之问	**Crossing River Han**　Song Zhiwen
岭外音书断， 经冬复历春。 近乡情更怯， 不敢问来人。	News cut off from beyond the mountain, all the year round through winter & spring. Timidity grows as I approach my home: I dare not ask questions from anybody. （张智中　译）

后来，读到英文句子：

His shyness got the better of him.

他害羞得不敢开口。

觉得如果用来翻译"近乡情更怯"，该有良好效果。改译如下：

Crossing River Han　Song Zhiwen

News cut off from beyond the mountain,

all the year round, from winter to spring

and onward. My growing timidity

gets the better of me, as I

approach my home: I

dare not inquire

about anything

from anybody.

（张智中　译）

"很多年以后回到家乡，是怎样的感觉？大概都被'近乡情更怯'这一句说完了。家乡是自己从小长大的地方，有熟悉的环境，有熟悉的人。很多年没有回去，沧海桑田，家里有哪些变化了？亲人们有什么消息了？别人会怎么看远离了多年的自己？近乡原本应该欣喜，此时因着这些牵绊，却心生忐忑，心生怯意了。真的是这样，哪一个远离家乡的人，没有体验到这样一种心情的？"[29]比较下面三个译文：

After Crossing Hanjiang River　Song Zhiwen

While being in Lingnan I received no letter,

The spring comes again aft went away the winter.

I fear more when coming to the hometown nearby,

Ask those who walk up to me even not dare I.

（冯志杰　译）[30]

Crossing the Han River

The ranges bar from home all news;

Winter spells elapse to spring hues.

As my desired hometown looms nigh,

I dare not ask a passer-by.

（赵彦春　译）[31]

Crossing River Han　Song Zhiwen

I longed for news on the frontier

From day to day, from year to year.

Now nearing home, timid I grow;

I dare not ask what I would know.

（许渊冲　译）[32]

"近乡情更怯，不敢问来人。"上引三个译文分别是：

I fear more when coming to the hometown nearby, \ Ask those who walk up to me even not dare I。这里的 fear（害怕；恐惧），用词过当。

As my desired hometown looms nigh, \ I dare not ask a passer-by。这里的 desired，用词偏颇。

Now nearing home, timid I grow; \ I dare not ask what I would

29 谢韩，讲给孩子的唐宋诗 [M]，成都：四川人民出版社，2019：244-246。

30 冯志杰，唐诗绝句 100 首 [Z]，北京：当代中国出版社，2019：21。

31 赵彦春，英韵唐诗百首 [Z]，北京：高等教育出版社，2019：37。

32 许渊冲，唐诗三百首：汉英对照 [Z]，北京：海豚出版社，2013：20。

know。这里，timid（胆怯的），也不是"近乡情更怯"中"怯"的真正含义。

我们借鉴英文句子而来的表达：My growing timidity gets the better of me，不仅达意，而且英文惟妙惟肖，生动传神。

（32）田家春望（李白）

田家春望　李白	**Spring View of the Field**　Li Bai
出门何所见？ 春色满平芜。 可叹无知己， 高阳一酒徒。	Away from home, what do you see? Spring fills the even field. Alas, without a bosom friend, a drunkard of Gaoyang. （张智中　译）

最近读到一句英文：

… and heaved a broken sigh.

时不时还叹口气。

句子看起来简单，但形容词 broken 与名词 sigh 的搭配，却令人感到鲜活生动。改译如下：

Spring View of the Field　Li Bai

Out of the door and away from home,

what do you see? A stretch of green,

an expanse of spring, fills the field.

Without a bosom friend, I, a lonely

drunkard of Gaoyang,

heave a broken

sigh upon

sigh.

（张智中　译）

（33）春怨（刘方平）

春怨　刘方平 纱窗日落渐黄昏， 金屋无人见泪痕。 寂寞空庭春欲晚， 梨花满地不开门。	**Spring Complaint**　Liu Fangping The sunlight on gauze window fades and dusk descends; in the sumptuous house, nobody sees my streaming tears. The lonely courtyard sees spring fading and dying; pear blossoms blanket the ground, no mood to open the door. （张智中　译）

读到这么一个英文句子：

Dusky twilight was giving place to deeper shadows, …
暗夜逐渐笼罩了朦胧的晚霞。

形容词 dusky 与名词 twilight 的搭配，出人意表之外；细品，却觉得深有回味之余地。接下来的 giving place to deeper shadows（让步于更深的影子），汉语简直无法译出。借鉴之后，《春怨》改译如下：

Spring Complaint　Liu Fangping

The sunlight on gauze window fades as dusky

twilight is giving place to deeper shadows ….

In the sumptuous house, nobody sees

my streaming tears. The lonely

courtyard sees spring fading

and dying; pear blossoms

blanket the ground, no

mood to open

the door.

（张智中　译）

后来，又读到两个英文句子：

When the sun was going down, …
太阳落山时。

He moved from end to end of his **voluptuous** bedroom, looking

—89—

again at the scraps of the day's journey that came unbidden into his mind.

他在自己富丽堂皇的卧室里来回走动着，不由自主地回想起白天旅行时遇到的种种情景。

那么，"纱窗日落渐黄昏"的英译，似乎可前置 When the sun is going down …；"金屋无人见泪痕"之"金屋"，若用定语 voluptuous（激起性欲的；沉溺酒色的；撩人的），当比 sumptuous（华丽的；奢侈的）更合适，更契合《春怨》之内涵。因此，《春怨》再次改译如下：

Spring Complaint   Liu Fangping

When the sun is going down the sunlight is caught

on the gauze window, as dusky twilight is

giving place to deeper shadows …

In the voluptuous house, nobody

sees my streaming tears. The

lonely courtyard sees spring

fading and dying, when

pear blossoms blanket

the ground, no mood

to open the door.

（张智中　译）

（34）自遣（李白）

对酒不觉暝，落花盈我衣。

醉起步溪月，鸟还人亦稀。

原　译	改　译
Self Abandonment　Li Bai Drinking and drinking, unaware of gloaming; falling petals fill the fold of my clothes. In drunken steps, I walk along the stream glittering with moonlight;	**Self Abandonment**　Li Bai Drinking off glass after glass, in a cool and pleasing air, as the evening darkens and comes on with expansive gloaming, I sit alone, while falling petals fill the fold of my clothes. My homeward journey, in drunken steps, is undertaken alone, along the stream silvery with moonlight: birds gone,

birds gone, people barely seen. （张智中　译）	the crowd dilute to a few passers-by, whose forms begin to grow dim. （张智中　译）

改译中，in a cool and pleasing air，来自下面英文句子：

> After they had dined **in a cool and pleasing air**, they began to dance.
> 在清爽宜人的环境中吃过饭后，便开始跳舞。

As the evening darkens and comes on with expansive gloaming，来自如下英语诗行：

I lean back, **as the evening darkens and comes on**. A chicken hawk floats over, looking for home. I have wasted my life.	我仰身向后，当暝色四合， 一只幼鹰滑过，寻找他的家。 我已经虚度了一生。 （赵毅衡　译）³³

"暝色四合"，又令人想起"对酒不觉暝"：the evening darkens and comes on 的表述，用上，则诗意大增。

I sit alone，来自英文：

> Maureen sat alone as the dark fell, while neon lights came on across
> the hills and bled pools of amber into the night.
> 莫琳就这样一个人坐着，坐了许久。直到夜幕降临，华灯初上，
> 琥珀色的灯光映入夜空。

My homeward journey, in drunken steps, is undertaken alone 源于：

> My journey to Paris **was not undertaken alone**.
> 我不是独自去的巴黎。

随后，the crowd dilute to a few passers-by, whose forms begin to grow dim，源于：

> They switched off their CD player and packed away their things, and
> **the crowd diluted to a few passers-by**.
> 围观的人群渐渐散去，又成了陌路人。

---

33 晏榕，诗的复活：诗意现实的现代构成与新诗学——美国现当代诗歌论衡及引申
　　[M]，杭州：浙江大学出版社，2013：185。

以及：

> The twilight deepened till their forms began to grow dim.
> 暮色渐浓，他们的形体渐渐变得模糊起来。

后来，又读到两句英文：

> Late that night, once they'd made sure that Auntie was all right, **people began to disperse in twos and threes**.
> 人们才三三两两散去。

这不正是"鸟还人亦稀"的状貌吗？

> **By imperceptible degrees**, he had become known among the people.
> 不知不觉，人们渐渐了解了他。

觉得"不知不觉"的英文 by imperceptible degrees 大好。

以及霍克斯英译《红楼梦》第七回中一个句子的英译：

> 二人计议已定，那天气已是掌灯时分，出来又看他们玩了一回牌。

> They had concluded their discussion **in gathering dusk**, and now moved back into the lamplit outer room and watched the ladies at their cards for a while.

"掌灯时分"，英译为 in gathering dusk，语言鲜活。

如果运用这三处英文，李白《自遣》可再次改译如下。首先，散体排列：

Self Abandonment　Li Bai

> I sit, as the evening darkens and comes on with expansive gloaming by imperceptible degrees, daylight on the disappearing, alone in a cool and pleasing air, drinking off glass after glass, while falling petals fill the fold of my clothes. My homeward journey, in drunken steps, and in gathering dusk, is undertaken alone, along the stream silvery with moonlight: birds gone, the crowd begin to disperse in twos and threes, diluting to a few passers-by, whose forms begin to grow dim.

读来已是很好的英文散文。在一字不改的情况下，诗体排列如下：

Self Abandonment　Li Bai

I sit, as the evening darkens and comes on with expansive gloaming

by imperceptible degrees, daylight on the disappearing, alone in

a cool and pleasing air, drinking off glass after glass, while

falling petals fill the fold of my clothes. My homeward

journey, in drunken steps, and in gathering dusk,

is undertaken alone, along the stream

silvery with moonlight: birds gone,

the crowd begin to disperse

in twos and threes, diluting

to a few passers-by,

whose forms

begin to

grow

dim.

（张智中　译）

不妨比较许渊冲的英译：

Solitude　Li Bai

I'm drunken with wine

And with moonshine,

With flowers fallen o'er the ground

And o'er me the blue-gowned.

Sobered, I stroll along the stream

Whose ripples gleam.

I see no bird

And hear no word.[34]

在许渊冲多达千首的古诗英译中，这首是个例外：没有以四行译四行，而是翻译成了八行，也没有追求每行音节数量的一致。但是，译诗的效果，却是非常好的。开头两行就富于诗意：I'm drunken with wine / And with moonshine（我醉了酒，也醉了月色）。接下来，With flowers fallen o'er the ground / And

34 许渊冲，唐诗三百首：汉英对照［Z］，北京：海豚出版社，2013：63-64。

o'er me the blue-gowned（花儿落在地上，也落在我蓝色的衣服上）。英文里的 blue（蓝色）有闷闷不乐之意，因有《自遣》。整体而言，译诗非常之好，可谓许渊冲的成功之译。

然而，与上引"繁冗"之译相比，许译却又似乎显得单薄寡味了。再看翁显良的译诗：

At Peace　Li Bai

Didn't know night had fallen — flowers too — fallen all over me.

Sobering up now. Up and take a stroll, along the gleaming stream.

Not a bird out, hardly anyone, just the moon and me. The moon. And me.[35]

首句英译，无主语，属于异化翻译。其次，"我衣"之"衣"，省译，乃是无关大局之细节。"溪月"译为 gleaming stream，"月"字未译，却以 gleaming（月亮之闪光）出之，乃深层之译。译诗之结尾，深有余味。译者之创造性，于此显见。宇文所安的英译：

My Feelings

Facing my wine, unaware of darkness growing,

Falling flowers cover my robes.

Drunk I rise, step on the moon in the creek —

Birds are turning back now,

men too are growing fewer.

显然，译文对原文，亦步亦趋，有时难免过分。比如"步溪月"的英译 step on the moon in the creek——人如何踩在溪流中的月亮之上？

韦利的英译：

Self-Abandonment

I sat drinking and did not notice the dusk,

Till falling petals filled the folds of my dress.

Drunken I rose and walked to the moonlit stream,

The birds were gone, and men also few.

（Arthur D. Waley 译）[36]

---

35 翁显良，古诗英译 [Z]，北京：北京出版社，1985：21。

36 江岚，唐诗西传史论——以唐诗在英美的传播为中心 [M]，北京：学苑出版社，2009：133。

语言流畅，表意清晰，可谓文从字顺。小畑熏良的英译：

THE SOLITUDE OF NIGHT

It was at a wine party —

I lay in a drowse, knowing it not.

The blown flowers fell and filled my lap.

When I arose, still drunken,

The birds had all gone to their nests,

And there remained but few of my comrades.

I went along the river — alone in the moonlight.

（Shigeyoshi Obata 译）

显然，a wine party 的变通，第三行中 flowers，fell，filled 的头韵使用，along 与 alone 的音似而意远之效果，都使得小畑熏良的译文更有味道。难怪曾在美国轰动一时，引众人捧读。不过，与之前我们读英文之后英译的《自遣》，似乎又显得有点局促。

（35）山中与幽人对酌（李白）

眼里读着英文，心里想着古诗，有时可改进译文。例如读到这样的英文句子：

And soon **a light, pleasant drowsiness came upon him**.

很快，一阵轻松而又舒适的睡意便涌了上来。

想起"我醉欲眠卿且去"的英译：

山中与幽人对酌　李白 两人对酌山花开， 一杯一杯复一杯。 我醉欲眠卿且去， 明朝有意抱琴来。	**Drinking with a Recluse in the Mountain**　Li Bai Mountain flowers abloom, we two are drinking off glass after glass. I am drunk and on the point of sleep: you may leave now and, come back tomorrow, if you please, with your Chinese lute. （张智中　译）

于是，改译如下：

Drinking with a Recluse in the Mountain　　Li Bai

Mountain flowers abloom, we are drinking

off glass after glass, you and me, until

a light, pleasant drowsiness comes

upon me. I am on the point of

sleep　—　you may leave

now and, come back

tomorrow, if you

please, with your

Chinese

lute.

（张智中　译）

"我醉欲眠"，原译 I am drunk and on the point of sleep，似乎已经很好。但改译 until a light, pleasant drowsiness comes upon me. I am on the point of sleep（一阵轻松而又舒适的睡意拥了上来），语气更加微妙到位。短语 on the point of，意为"就要……之际；正要……之际"。霍克斯英译《红楼梦》第十三回有过运用：

不知不觉已交三鼓，平儿已睡熟了。凤姐方觉睡眼微蒙，恍惚只见秦氏从外走进来。

By this time Patience was fast asleep and Xi-feng herself was **on the point of** dropping off when she became dimly aware that Qin-shi had just walked into the room from outside.

另外，we are drinking off glass after glass，来自如下英文：

I could hear him clear his throat and sigh as **he drank off glass after glass**.

他一边叹着气，一边一杯接一杯地喝酒。

（36）登乐游原（李商隐）

登乐游原	Ascending the Pleasure Plateau
向晚意不适，	Being out of sorts

驱车登古原。 夕阳无限好， 只是近黄昏。	towards the eve, I drive a chariot to the ancient plateau. The beauty of the setting sun knows no bounds, but alas, it is declining and closing. （张智中　译）

其中，being out of sorts 来自这个英文句子：

I've been **feeling rather out of sorts** lately.

我最近感觉不大对劲。

后来，又读到两个描写太阳落山的英文句子：

The sun, already well down, hurried its descent into the water.

夕阳已落到很低的地方，以越来越快的速度向水里沉下去。

The sun dipped **below the horizon**.

太阳落到地平线下了。

于是改译：

Ascending the Pleasure Plateau　Li Shangyin

Being out of sorts towards evening, I

drive a chariot to the ancient plateau.

The sun, whose beauty knows no

bounds, is already well

down, hurrying its

descent below

the horizon.

（张智中　译）

再读英文：

As **the evening was drawing to a close** his friends finally persuaded him to write a little music in honour of the happy occasion they had all shared.

When you're settled, take a few minutes to think back over a time of soulful sadness that has finished or **is drawing to a close**.

《登乐游原》另译：

Ascending the Pleasure Plateau　Li Shangyin

Being out of sorts towards the eve,

I drive a chariot to the ancient

plateau. The beauty of the

setting sun knows no

bounds, only it is

drawing to a

close.

（张智中　译）

后来，又读到两个类似的英文句子：

By this time the gentle winds began to blow, and **the sun grew near to setting**.

这时微风轻起，太阳即将下山。

The king then lifted his eyes to Heaven, and seeing **the sun begin to fall low**, he thus spoke.

这时，国王抬起头来注视天空，见太阳已经西沉，便说道。

这里的英文：the sun grew near to setting 和 the sun begin(s) to fall low，简单却富有英文之味道。虽然上引之改译已比较满意，若运用这两个句子中的英文表达，可再次改译如下：

Ascending the Pleasure Plateau　Li Shangyin

When the sun, growing near to setting,

begins to fall low, I, feeling out of sorts,

drive a chariot to the ancient plateau.

The sun, whose beauty knows no

bounds, is already well

down, hurrying its

descent below

the horizon.

（张智中　译）

最近又读到两个相关的英文短语或句子：

Late in the afternoon, …

傍晚时分。

And as **the dim ball of the sun sank slowly into** the northwest …

当太阳暗淡的圆球慢慢地沉入西北方时……

第一个，late in the afternoon 看似简单，却有余味。第二个，the dim ball of the sun sank slowly into …，这里的头韵很好，而且，"太阳暗淡的圆球"之意象，鲜明而确切。因此，尝试再译《登乐游原》，散体如下：

Late in the afternoon, as the dim ball of the sun is sinking slowly in the horizon, I feel out of sorts and drive a chariot to the ancient plateau where the sunny beauty knows no bounds before it fades to be fainter, paler, and dimmer ….

诗体排列如下：

Ascending the Pleasure Plateau　Li Shangyin

Late in the afternoon, as the dim ball of the sun

is sinking slowly in the horizon, I feel

out of sorts and drive a chariot

to the ancient plateau where

the sunny beauty knows

no bounds before it

fades to be fainter,

paler, and

dimmer

….

（张智中　译）

整首诗的诗行，全部居中排列，呈现一定的形状，这在当代英文诗歌里是比较常见的。在不改动如上译诗，包括标点符号，都不做任何改变的情况下，仅仅改动诗行排列，可得如下另外两种译诗：

Ascending the Pleasure Plateau　Li Shangyin Late in the afternoon, as the dim ball of the sun is sinking slowly in the horizon, I feel out of sorts and drive a chariot to the ancient plateau where the sunny beauty knows no bounds before it fades to be fainter, paler, and dimmer … （张智中　译）	**Ascending the Pleasure Plateau**　Li Shangyin Late in the afternoon, 　　as the dim ball of 　　　the sun is sinking slowly in the horizon, 　　I feel out of sorts 　　　and drive a chariot to the ancient plateau 　　where the sunny 　　　beauty knows no bounds before it 　　fades to be fainter, 　　　paler, and dimmer …. （张智中　译）

　　左边的译文，保持原文的四行，中规中矩；右边的译文，三行对原文的一行，每三行一个单元，逐行缩进，这是西方译者较为常见的译诗形式。虽然内容，包括标点，完全相同，但不同的诗行排列，会带来不同的视觉效果和阅读效果。

　　"只是近黄昏"，英译为 it fades to be fainter, paler, and dimmer，用了三个 -er 比较级的形容词，来描写天色渐黄昏的过程，比较生动形象。其实，灵感来源于多年前读到的一首英文短诗：

Night　Max Webber

Fainter, dimmer, stiller each moment,

Now night.

　　此诗之妙，就在于三个 -er 比较级形容词的运用。

　　李商隐《登乐游原》已经好几个译文了，但是，我们又读到英文名著 The Great Gatsby 中的句子：

For a moment the last sunshine fell with romantic affection upon her glowing face; her voice compelled me forward breathlessly as I listened — then **the glow faded, each light deserting her with lingering regret, like children leaving a pleasant street at dusk**.

　　在那一刻，最后一缕阳光让她炽热的脸庞溢满了浪漫的情感，她的声音将我逼迫我向前，直至无法呼吸——然后，光芒渐渐褪去，每一束光都将她遗失在悠长的后悔中，就像孩子在黄昏时恋恋不舍地离开愉快的街道。

以及 *Gone with the Wind* 中的一个句子：

> She was done with marriage but not with love, for her love for Ashley was something different, having nothing to do with passion or marriage, something sacred and **breathtakingly beautiful**, an emotion that grew stealthily through the long days of her enforced silence, feeding on oft-thumbed memories and hopes.

> 思嘉与结婚这件事已经不相干了，但与恋爱则并非如此，因为她对艾希礼的爱情是不一样的，那是与情欲或婚姻没有关系的，是一种神圣而十分惊人地美丽的东西，一种在长期被压迫默不作声，但时常靠回忆希望来维持着的过程中偷偷增长的激情。

借鉴之后，《登乐游原》又译如下，并回译成汉语：

Ascending the Pleasure Plateau Li Shangyin Being out of sorts towards the eve, I drive a chariot to the ancient plateau. Breathtakingly beautiful is the setting sun whose last beams fade into a glow, each light deserting the world with lingering regret, like children leaving a pleasant street at dusk. （张智中　译）	登乐游原　李商隐 傍晚时分，略感不适， 驾车兜风，来到古原。 落日呈现惊人之美—— 最后一缕阳光，退烧 退热，退出这个 世界，恋恋不舍， 就像孩子离开 愉快的街衢， 在黄昏。 （张智中　译）

后来，竟然又读到一首英译及其汉译：

The Night James Carew The night is sliding down the rainbow To meet the red sunset The sunset will give light but not for long, For night has come again With the darkness.	夜晚　詹姆斯·卡鲁 夜从彩虹身上悄悄溜下， 去见红红的夕阳。 夕阳仍有余辉， 只是不会久长。 夜幕再次降临， 又是漆黑一片。[37]

那么，借鉴之后，李商隐《登乐游原》又有新译：

---

37 刘文杰，英语诗歌汉译与赏析［M］，广州：中山大学出版社，2014：236。

Ascending the Pleasure Plateau　Li Shangyin

Being out of sorts late in the afternoon, I drive a chariot

to the ancient plateau where my gaze completes a circle

of the world about me: what a glorious spectacle!

The sun is beginning to sink slowly into

a dim ball, when the night is sliding

down the rainbow to meet the red

sunset, which will give light

but not for long.

（张智中　译）

读英文：

Since we **complete a circle** around the sun every year, the stars of summer, such as those in the Big Dipper, are always the stars of summer.

由于每年绕着太阳完成一个循环，夏日里我们所看到的星星，比如北斗七星，它们始终在其他年份的夏天里也都能看得到。

Nell gazed in silence on the **glorious spectacle**.

内尔静静地盯着这壮丽的景色。

He **was alive to** every new scene, joyful when he saw **the beauties of the setting sun**, and more happy when he beheld it rise and recommence a new day.

每个新景色都令他兴致盎然，夕阳之美令他欢喜；旭日东升更令他快乐，因为新的一天开始了。

His tale had occupied the whole day, and the sun **was upon the verge of the horizon** when he departed.

他整整讲了一天的故事，当他离开时，太阳已经快落山了。

The deep grief **which this scene had at first excited quickly gave way to** rage and despair.

起初，此景激起了我深深的悲痛，但很快就被愤怒和绝望所取代了。

Night quickly shut in, but to my extreme wonder, I found that the cottagers had a means of prolonging light by the use of tapers, and was delighted to find that **the setting of the sun did not put an end to the pleasure I experienced in watching** my human neighbours.

　　夜幕很快降临了，我异常惊讶地发现，他们竟可以用蜡烛照亮，我欣喜地发现，虽然太阳落山了，可这并未妨碍我观察自己的人类邻居时所体验到的乐趣。

再译李商隐《登乐游原》，首先散译：

Ascending the Pleasure Plateau　　Li Shangyin

　　Being out of sorts towards evening, I drive a chariot to the ancient plateau where my gaze completes a circle of the world about me: what a glorious spectacle! I am alive to the new scene, joyful at the beauties of the setting sun which is upon the verge of the horizon, but the admiration which this scene has excited quickly gives way to a growing sense of gloom, when the setting of the sun seems to put an end to the pleasure I experience in watching it.

　　　　（张智中　译）

诗行排列后，如下：

Ascending the Pleasure Plateau　　Li Shangyin

Being out of sorts towards evening,

　　I drive a chariot to the ancient plateau

　　　　where my gaze completes a circle

of the world about me: what a glorious

　　spectacle! I am alive to the new scene,

　　　　joyful at the beauties of the setting sun

which is upon the verge of the horizon,

　　but the admiration which this scene

　　　　has excited quickly gives way to

a growing sense of gloom, when the

　　setting of the sun seems to put an end to

　　　　the pleasure I experience in watching it.

　　　　（张智中　译）

再读英文:

Upon the bank of the Nile **at eventide**, a hyena met a crocodile and they stopped and greeted one another.

黄昏时分,一只土狼在尼罗河岸上遇到一条鳄鱼,他们停下步来,互相致意。

If I were to choose **a spot from which the rising or setting sun could be seen to the greatest possible advantage**, it would be from this neighborhood.

如果我要选择一个看日出日落的最佳地点,那就是这里。

The maiden **turned her eyes eastward**.

这位少女将视线转向东方。

Harry, keeping close beside her, **observed her with anxious interest**.

哈里紧紧地跟在内尔旁边,担忧地注视着她。

A faint streak of pale rose tinted the light vapors of the horizon. It was **the first ray of light attacking the laggards of the night**.

一道淡淡的浅玫瑰色给地平线上薄薄的蒸汽着了一层色。这第一缕光线赶走了夜晚。

Would the first beams of day **overpower her feelings**?

白天的第一束光亮会让她受不了吗?

A faint streak of pale rose tinted the light vapors of the horizon.

一道淡淡的浅玫瑰色给地平线上薄薄的蒸汽着了一层色。

His only grief had been to perceive the bed becoming impoverished, and to see the hour approaching when the seam would be exhausted.

他仅有的悲痛便是意识到煤床变得贫瘠、目睹着煤层枯竭的时刻渐渐临近。

借鉴如上英文表达,《登乐游原》散文英译如下:

Ascending the Pleasure Plateau　　Li Shangyin

Feeling out of sorts at eventide, I drive a chariot to the ancient plateau, a spot from which the setting sun can be seen to the greatest possible advantage. I turn my eyes westward, to see a sun which is growing near to setting, and I observe it with anxious interest. It is already well down, hurrying its descent, when the last rays of light are attacking the laggards of the day. The beauty from the last beams of day, which knows no bounds, overpowers my feelings, when a faint streak of pale rose is tinting the light vapors of the horizon. Oh, the day, gorgeous and splendid, is declining and closing. My only grief is to see the hour approaching — when the slanting sun would drop itself behind the mountains.

（张智中　译）

诗体排列如下：

Ascending the Pleasure Plateau　Li Shangyin

Feeling out of sorts at eventide,

 I drive a chariot to the ancient

  plateau, a spot from which the

setting sun can be seen to the greatest

 possible advantage. I turn my eyes

  westward, to see a sun which is

growing near to setting, and I

 observe it with anxious interest.

  It is already well down, hurrying

its descent, when the last rays of

 light are attacking the laggards of

  the day. The beauty from the last

beams of day, which knows no bounds,

 overpowers my feelings, when

  a faint streak of pale rose is tinting

the light vapors of the horizon.

 Oh, the day, gorgeous and splendid,

  is declining and closing. My only

grief is to see the hour approaching

— when the slanting sun would

    drop itself behind the mountains.

（张智中　译）

比较许渊冲的英译：

On the Plain of Tombs　Li Shangyin

At dusk my heart is filled with gloom;

I drive my cab to ancient tomb.

The setting sun seems so sublime,

But it is near its dying time.[38]

显而易见，许渊冲的英译，是追求音形意三美的传统译诗，而我们不仅借鉴英文，而且有大胆的想象和添加，给译文注入了新诗的元素与活力。

"有些翻译在语法上是完美的、没有漏洞，但却没有'英语味'。"[39]这基本上是中国人做汉译英的一个通病。译文必须有英语味，译文才能给读者以美感，读者才会喜欢。

（37）回乡偶书二首（一）（贺知章）

回乡偶书二首（一）	Returning Home (No. 1 of two poems)
少小离家老大回， 乡音无改鬓毛衰。 儿童相见不相识， 笑问客从何处来。	I left my home young and returned old; though hair gray, unchanged is my accent. I'm a stranger to the children here; beaming, they ask: "where are you from, dear sir?" （张智中　译）

英文小说《飘》（*Gone with the Wind*）里的句子：

As a child, she often had crept to the door and, peeping through the

tiniest crack, had seen Ellen emerge from the dark room.

那时她还很小，常常爬到门口去，从狭窄的门缝里窥望，看到

---

38 许渊冲，唐诗三百首：汉英对照［Z］，北京：海豚出版社，2013：191。

39 徐晓飞、房国铮，翻译与文化：翻译中的文化建构［M］，上海：上海交通大学出版社，2019：97。

爱伦从黑暗的房间里出来。

"I'll go now and find your father," he said, **smiling all over his face**.

"我现在就去找你父亲，"他喜气洋洋地说。

Uncle Henry was a short, pot-bellied, irascible old gentleman with a pink face, **a shock of long silver hair** and an utter lack of patience with feminine timidities and vaporings.

亨利叔叔是个性情暴戾老绅士，矮个儿，大肚子，脸孔红红的，一头蓬乱的银白长发，他非常看不惯那种女性的怯弱和爱说大话的习惯。

He looked down at her **radiantly**, **his whole clean simple heart in his eyes**.

可是他却笑容满面地俯视着她，仿佛他那颗洁净而单纯的心已完整地反映在他的眼光中。

又，其它地方见到的表达：

... **a genuine smile on someone's face**, ...

汲取上引英文精华，《回乡偶书》改译如下：

Returning Home (No. 1 of two poems)　　He Zhizhang

I left home as a boy and returned an old man

with a shock of long silver hair; my accent

persists. I am a stranger to the children

who, a genuine smile all over their

faces, ask me radiantly, their

whole clean simple heart

in their eyes, "where

are you from,

dear sir?"

（张智中　译）

又读到《飘》（*Gone with the Wind*）里的这个句子：

"I want to know all about the County," she said, **beaming upon him**.

"我很想听听县里所有的情况，"她笑容满面地对他说。

《回乡偶书》另译如下：

Returning Home (No. 1 of two poems)　He Zhizhang

I left home as a boy and returned an old man

with a shock of long silver hair; my accent

persists. I am a stranger to the children

who, beaming upon me, ask innocently,

"where are you from, dear sir?"

their whole clean simple

heart in their eyes.

（张智中　译）

读到英文：

A goat was **looking at me with innocent eyes**.

一只山羊用孩童般的目光打量着我。

His hands over his mouth, Dongsha **responded with the innocence of a child**: "Yes, Ma'am!"

东沙捂着自己的嘴，一脸孩子气地说，知道了，夫人。

《回乡偶书》另译如下：

Returning Home (No. 1 of two poems)　He Zhizhang

I left my home young and now return old; with

silver-streaked hair, unchanged is my accent.

I am a stranger to the children about me,

who, beaming and looking at me

with innocent eyes, ask:

"where are you from,

dear sir?"

（张智中　译）

原译 though hair gray，失之平淡，改译 with silver-streaked hair，形象鲜明；原译 I am a stranger to the children here，这里的 here，显得笼统，改成 about me，孩子们围着"我"，前呼后拥的形象就产生了。原译 beaming, they ask，改为 who, beaming and looking at me with innocent eyes, ask，译文便有了画面感。当然，第二个英文句子中 with the innocence of a child（带着孩子般的天真），诗中描写的本是孩子，所以就没有用上。若描写成人而具孩子般的天真，则可

排上用场。读英文而处处留心，译文总会有所进步。

后来，又读到《飘》（*Gone with the Wind*）中这样一个英文句子：

The prospect looked brighter to Scarlett, so bright in fact that she **turned beaming eyes on** Charles and **smiled from pure joy**.

这时思嘉的前景已显得更加明朗，事实上已明朗得叫她回过头来，用纯粹出于喜悦的心情向查尔斯嫣然一笑。

《回乡偶书》又译如下：

Returning Home (No. 1 of two poems)　　He Zhizhang

I left home as a boy and returned as an old man;

in spite of silver-streaked hair, my accent

persists. I am a stranger to the children

about me, who, turning beaming

eyes on me and smiling from

pure joy, ask me radiantly,

their whole clean simple

heart in their eyes,

"where are you

from, dear

sir?"

（张智中　译）

读英文：

In spite of my entrance, her attitude strangely **persisted**.

尽管我已进来了，她却纹丝不动。

Her hair is tinged with grey.

她的头发有些花白。

It was Flora who, **gazing all over me in candid wonder**, was the first. She was struck with our bareheaded aspect.

弗洛拉如此率直地、充满好奇地盯着我全身看还是第一次。

His age may have been nearer forty than thirty, but his cheeks were so ruddy and **his eyes so merry that he still conveyed the impression of** a plump and mischievous boy.

他虽然已经快四十岁了，但脸色红润，目光欢快，仍然给人一种淘气的胖男孩印象。

《回乡偶书》英译：

Returning Home (No. 1 of two poems)　　He Zhizhang

I left home as a boy
　　and returned as an old
　　　　man, whose native accent
persists, though my hair
　　is heavily tinged with
　　　　grey. The children, gazing
all over me in candid
　　wonder, ask me: "where
　　　　are you from, dear sir?"
Their eyes so merry that
　　they convey the impression
　　　　of mischievous boys & girls.

（张智中　译）

比较许渊冲的英译：

Home-Coming　　He Zhizhang

I left home young and not till old do I come back,
Unchanged my accent, my hair no longer black.
My children whom I meet do not know who am I.
"Where do you come from, sir? " they ask with beaming eye.[40]

我们英文读多了，便会感觉到许渊冲译诗中，有时似乎有点油滑的味道。汉诗英译，要有英语的味道，就像英诗汉译，应该有汉语诗歌的味道，是一个道理。

（38）夜宿山寺（李白）

读到这样一个英文句子：

From the depth of the canyon comes welling silence. Seldom can

---

40 许渊冲，唐诗三百首：汉英对照 [Z]，北京：海豚出版社，2013：22。

you hear the roar of the river, you cannot catch the patter. Like applause, from the leaves of the cottonwoods on the shelf-like plateau below you. For all sounds are swallowed in this gulf of space. **"It makes one want to murmur."**

沉寂从深谷中升腾上来，你听不到谷底河流的咆哮，谷底梯状高原上三叶杨的沙沙声像是有人在鼓掌，你也听不到，所有的声音都淹没在这空旷之中。"在这里都不敢高声说话啊"。

其中，It makes one want to murmur，语言虽然简单，却深有余味。"在这里都不敢高声说话啊"，似乎正是李白《夜宿山寺》中"不敢高声语"的白话译文。读之惊喜，因有改译。

原　诗	原　译	改　译
夜宿山寺 危楼高百尺， 手可摘星辰。 不敢高声语， 恐惊天上人。	**Spending Night in a Mountain Temple** The temple stands high heavenward; a traveler's hands may reach the stars. He dares not speak aloud, lest people in paradise be disturbed. （张智中　译）	**Spending Night in a Mountain Temple** The temple towers heavenward; a traveler's hands may reach the stars. It makes one want to murmur, lest people in paradise be disturbed. （张智中　译）

后来，又读到英文：

Success is within reach and the chances for promotion **are close at hand.**

眼看就要出成绩了，就要有选拔的机会了。

The sky was so clear and black, **it throbbed with stars**, and the moon was losing its fullness once more.

夜幕漆黑孤清，微弱地闪着星光，月亮又缺了。

这两个句子，令人联想到"手可摘星辰"，似可译为：the sky which, throbbing with stars, is within reach and the twinkling stars are quite close at hand.（天空，微弱地闪着星光，咫尺之遥，闪烁的星星伸手可及。）

She imagined she could hear the stars. She imagined distinctly she

could hear the celestial, musical motion of the stars, quite near at hand.

她想她可以听到天上的星星絮语，听到星星奏着乐在附近翱翔。

这里，the celestial, musical motion of the stars，对应译文"星星奏着乐"，只是意译。如果直而译之，该是："星星那天上的、音乐般的转动。"极富诗意。

总之，《夜宿山寺》再次改译如下：

Spending Night in a Mountain Temple　Li Bai

The imposing temple towers heavenward; the sky

which, throbbing with stars, is within reach and

the twinkling stars are quite close at hand.

It seems the celestial, musical motion

of the stars could be heard, and it

makes one want to murmur,

lest people in heaven

be disturbed.

（张智中　译）

不久，又读到一个英文句子：

He sat **beneath a hard night sky, alive with stars**.

他在繁星满天的夜空下歇息。

则《夜宿山寺》可另译如下：

Spending Night in a Mountain Temple　Li Bai

The imposing temple towers heavenward; the hard

night sky which, alive with stars, is within reach

and the twinkling stars are quite close at hand.

It seems the celestial, musical motion

of the stars could be heard, and it

makes one want to murmur,

lest people in heaven

be disturbed.

（张智中　译）

又读到两个英文句子：

Not a breath stirred the chill Arctic quiet.

寒冷的北极静悄悄的，连呼吸声都没有。

The shrieks and the cries were **audible** there, though subdued by the distance.

虽然距离很远，但那尖叫在这儿也还隐约可闻。

《夜宿山寺》用常见当代英诗形式另译如下，并比较许渊冲的英译：

Spending Night in a Mountain Temple Li Bai	The Summit Temple Li Bai
The imposing temple towers 　heavenward; the hard night 　　sky which, throbbing with stars, is within reach and 　the twinkling stars are quite 　　close at hand. Not a breath stirs the chill quiet: seemingly 　audible is the celestial, 　　musical motion of the stars, and it makes one want 　to murmur, lest people 　　in heaven be disturbed. 　（张智中　译）	Hundred feet high the Summit Temple stands, Where I could pluck the stars with my own hands. At dead of night I dare not speak aloud For fear of waking dwellers in the cloud.[41] 　（许渊冲　译）

（39）岭上逢久别者又别（权德舆）

| 岭上逢久别者又别　权德舆
十年曾一别，
征路此相逢。
马首向何处？
夕阳千万峰。 | Meeting and Parting a Friend of Long Absence Quan Deyu
Ten years ago we bid
farewell; now we chance
meet on the way. Where
will the horse head?
Myriads of hills
in the setting sun.
　（张智中　译） |

后来，读到两个相关的英文句子：

Far out on the horizon, the metal sea sparkled against the morning

---

41 许渊冲，李白诗选：汉英对照［Z］，长沙：湖南人民出版社，2007：203。

light.

目之所及，金属质感的海面在晨光中闪闪发亮。

The horizon was **a series of blue peaks** that Harold longed to climb. The sun hung high in the eastern sky, leaving the moon so pale it looked made of cloud.

前面是几座哈罗德很想攀过的蓝色山峰，太阳高高挂在东边，衬得另一头的月亮苍白如一团云雾。

借鉴后，改译如下：

Meeting and Parting a Friend of Long Absence   Quan Deyu

Ten years ago we bid farewell and, now

we chance meet on the way. Where

is the horse heading? —— far out

on the horizon, a series of blue

peaks upon peaks, which

are caught in

the setting

sun.

（张智中　译）

后来，又读到 Miss Read 小说 *Tyler's Row* 中的一个句子：

We **greeted each other with unusual enthusiasm, meeting in a foreign part so unexpectedly**.

《岭上逢久别者又别》另译如下：

Meeting and Parting a Friend of Long Absence   Quan Deyu

Ten years ago from each other we parted, now

we meet in a foreign part so unexpectedly.

After greeting each other with unusual

enthusiasm, our horses plod onward

in opposite directions: myriads

of hills are caught in

the setting sun.

（张智中　译）

（40）赏牡丹（刘禹锡）

赏牡丹　刘禹锡 庭前芍药妖无格， 池上芙蕖净少情。 唯有牡丹真国色， 花开时节动京城。	**Appreciating Peony Flowers**　Liu Yuxi The fair fragrant peonies in the yard lack strength of character; the elegant lotus flowers in the pool want coquetry. Only peony flowers boast reigning beauty: the whole capital, in blooming season, is thronged with appreciators. （张智中　译）

后来，读 Donna Dailey 写的 *Charles Dickens* 一书，见到这样两个句子：

It became **the talk of the town**, with Pickwick hats, coats, canes, and cigars all the rage.

Work was always **the focus of** Dickens's life. The compulsion to take on more projects never left him. He was driven not only by the money, but also by the pleasure of the work itself.

Miss Read 的英文小说 *Tyler's Row* 中的这个句子：

"Come and see the vegetable patch," said Peter, when Robert had finished **admiring the flowers**.

《赏牡丹》改译如下：

Admiring Peony Flowers　Liu Yuxi

Fair fragrant peonies in the yard lack strength

of character; elegant lotus flowers in the pool

want coquetry. In flowering season, only

peony flowers, with its reigning beauty,

become the talk of the capital,

and the focus of people's

life: admiring flowers

all the rage.

（张智中　译）

个别字词稍微改动，并采取当代英诗形式，可得如下译诗：

Admiring Peony Flowers　Liu Yuxi

The fair fragrant peonies

　　　in the yard lack

　　　　　strength of character;

the elegant lotus

　　　flowers in the pool

　　　　　want coquetry.

Only peony flowers

　　　boast reigning

　　　　　beauty —

the whole capital,

　　　in blooming season,

　　　　　is thronged with admirers.

（张智中　译）

（41）少年行（杜甫）

少年行　杜甫	**Outing of a Youngster**　Du Fu
马上谁家白面郎， 临阶下马坐人床。 不通姓氏粗豪甚， 指点银瓶索酒尝。	A fair-faced boy on the horseback dismounts haughtily and takes a seat carelessly and, without pronouncing his name, he straightforwardly points at the silver jug, demanding a taste of the wine within. （张智中　译）

译诗似乎已经比较流畅。然而，读到下面的英文句子或表达：

You're a **regular** little gentleman.

你是一位十足的小绅士。

…**in his young playdays**, …

孩提时代。

…but he **has no thoughts for** that.

但他根本没有想到这一点。

根据诗意，可改写为：

without thoughts for the price (of the wine)。

借鉴之后，《少年行》改译如下，并路易·艾黎的译文：

A Regular Rascal in His Young Playdays Du Fu	**Too Young** Du Fu
A fair-faced boy, in his young playdays, dismounts <div align=center>from the horseback haughtily and takes a seat</div><div align=center>carelessly and, without pronouncing his</div><div align=center>name, he straightforwardly points</div><div align=center>at the silver jug, demanding</div><div align=center>a taste of the wine within,</div><div align=center>without thoughts for</div><div align=center>the price.</div><div align=center>（张智中　译）</div>	Who is, I wonder mildly, This little pretty Whipper-snapper; jumping From his horse So cockily, sitting down Uninvited; too sure Of himself to say Who he is; haughtily Pointing to the silver Jug, demanding I pour Wine for him?[42] （路易·艾黎　译）

（42）拜新月（李端）

拜新月　李端	**Praying to A New Moon** Li Duan
开帘见新月， 即便下阶拜。 细语人不闻， 北风吹罗带。	When she rolls up the screen and sees the new moon, She descends the steps and begins to pray, No one hears what soft words pass her lips; The sash round her waist keeps fluttering in the north wind. （文殊、王晋熙、邓炎昌　译）[43]

译文语言散淡，几无亮点。读到下面的英文句子：

Her distress awoke a nausea in her body and s**he kept moving her lips in silent fervent prayer**.

眼睛一亮，kept moving her lips in silent fervent prayer，不正描写嘴唇翕动而默默祈祷的状貌吗？借鉴入诗，英译如下：

42　（新西兰）艾黎（Rewi Alley），杜甫诗选（汉英对照）[Z]，北京：外文出版社，
　　2001：231。

43　文殊、王晋熙、邓炎昌，唐宋绝句名篇英译 [Z]，北京：外语教学与研究出版社，
　　1995：69。

Praying to A New Moon　Li Duan

The rolled-up screen

　　reveals a new moon,

　　　when she walks down

the steps to pray. She

　　keeps moving her lips

　　　in silent prayer, while

the green sash round

　　her waist is fluttering

　　　in the north wind.

（张智中　译）

（43）示儿（陆游）

示儿　陆游	**My Will to My Son**　Lu You
死去原知万事空， 但悲不见九州同。 王师北定中原日， 家祭无忘告乃翁。	When I am dead, everything is empty; sorrowful: the nine states of China have not been unified. When the imperial army have recovered the north land, forget not, in family sacrifice, to tell your father this news in the nether world. （张智中　译）

随后，读到下面一些与《示儿》相关的英文句子：

Bad news certainly **traveled swiftly**.

一定是那个讨厌的消息迅速传开了。

… which was **a great cause of joy to me**.

这让我很高兴。

We were **in a luscious flow of spirits** and vastly merry.

我们一起聊得兴高采烈。

We men **are all in a fever of excitement**.

我们男人们都很兴奋。

We **were all wild with excitement** yesterday.

昨天我们都激动得不得了。

She **could hardly contain herself for excitement**.

她激动得几乎控制不住自己。

This **elated me**.

这让我很兴奋。

Ursula **was in raptures**.

厄秀拉高兴极了。

I got up **in raptures**.

我欣喜若狂地站了起来。

《示儿》改译如下：

My Will to My Son Lu You

Upon dying, I come to know everything is empty;

sorrowful: the nine states of China have not

been unified. When the imperial army have

recovered the north land, the news travels

swiftly, a great cause of joy to you, who

are in a luscious flow of spirits, or in

a fever of excitement for which

you can hardly contain yourself,

forget not, in family sacrifice,

to tell your father this news,

to elate me in raptures

in the nether world.

（张智中　译）

又，读到这句英文：

This brought her mind back to the nagging worry which had been her constant companion for the last week or two.

借鉴后，《示儿》英译：

This brings my mind back to the nagging worry which has been my constant companion for the greater part of my lifetime.

整首《示儿》另译如下：

My Will to My Son　Lu You

Upon dying, I know that everything turns empty; I can

hardly contain myself for sorrow: the nine states

of China have not been unified. This brings

my mind back to the nagging worry which

has been my constant companion for the

greater part of my lifetime. When the

imperial army has eventually recovered

the north land, forget not, in family

sacrifice, to tell your father this

news in the nether world,

which will be a great

cause of joy

to me.

（张智中　译）

比较此诗的另外两种英译：

Testament to My Son　Lu You	**Shown to My Son**　Lu You
After my death I know for me all hopes are vain,	That death means an end to all I know at heart,
But still I'm grieved to see our country not unite.	I feel sad because the land is torn apart.
When Royal Armies recover the Central Plain,	Once the royal troops recover all north China,
Do not forget to tell your Sire in sacred rite!	At my grave, do tell the news to me — your father.
（许渊冲　译）⁴⁴	（邢全臣　译）⁴⁵

"死去"，真的译成 After my death（在我死后）？死又能知道什么呢？其实，"死去"乃是即将去世弥留之际。另译：That death means an end to all I know at heart（死亡意味着我心中所知道的一切的结束），似乎不能吻合"死去原知万事空"之意。对于古诗的理解和翻译，即便是中国译者，也会一不小心便落入原文文字的桎梏里面而不自知。

44 许渊冲，宋元明清诗选：汉英对照［Z］，北京：海豚出版社，2013：76。
45 邢全臣，用英语欣赏国粹：英汉对照［Z］，北京：科学出版社，2008：217。